"...a searing look back at an era of double standards and cloistered perversion. The story centers on three emotionally charged girls and the painful initiations of the adult world. *Silent Cry* takes surprising twists and turns which keep the reader guessing to the very end."

—Cheryl Brown, ***Atlantic Book Club***

"Julie Bigg Veazey explores the ferment and contradictions of the 1950s at an elite boarding school. Like Muriel Spark's masterpiece, *The Prime of Miss Jean Brodie,* Veazey offers part social commentary, part moving character study, both urgent and tangible. *Silent Cry* signals the debut of a deft new talent."

—***New York Times*** bestselling author, Ellen Tanner Marsh

"Poignant, utterly convincing, Julie Bigg Veazey looks into the private world of prep school and privileged childhood in this suspenseful tale. The spicy, fast-paced storyline gains momentum as it hurls us toward a shocking finale."

—Robert Leigh Meek, ***Chemistry of Power***

"Heart wrenching...but the sweetness of trusting friendships, like sugar crystals left at the bottom of this afternoon's teacups, will linger, and make you cry."

—Susan Tremblay, ***Portland Stage Co.***

"*Silent Cry* draws us into the exquisite anxieties of adolescence in this empathetic and sharply observant novel where the genuine characters are funny, strange, and complex, spinning and weaving toward a conclusion with a macabre twist."

—Sally Michener, ***Visual Artist***

Silent Cry

Julie Bigg Veazey

Booksurge Publishing, LLC, A division of Amazon.com
North Charleston, South Carolina

Silent Cry is a work of fiction. Names, characters, places, and incidents are the product of the author's imagination and are used fictitiously. Any resemblance to actual events, locales, or persons, living or dead, is entirely coincidental.

ISBN Number: 1-4196-3696-0
Library of Congress Control Number: 2006904233

Cover Design: Ari Alexenberg (www.weeklyecho.com)
Cover Photograph: Laurens Holst
Author Photograph: Elan Alexenberg

To contact the author, e-mail: silentcrynovel@yahoo.com

Booksurge Publishing, LLC, A division of Amazon.com
North Charleston, South Carolina

Printed in the United States of America

Silent Cry

Acknowledgements:

My forever thanks to my family: Bill Veazey for his continued optimism, encouragement, and meticulous editing over a long period of time, Sharon Stevens, my most passionate and attentive advocate, for her incredible effort in research, critical feedback and tireless attention to detail, Ralph Stevens for his excellent story ideas, Julie Alexenberg for her encouragement and Barbara DeWall for proofing and formatting with finesse.

My endless gratitude to Mary Linn Roby for the insight she gave to the shaping of this novel and her editorial suggestions that brought it to publication. Additional thanks to Vicki Terrani for initial editing, Cheryl Brown and Sally Michener for their gracious enthusiasm, and to Elizabeth Knies, dear friend and fellow writer, my appreciation for her patience, discerning suggestions, and wise words: *keep going.*

To Bill,
Without your presence in my life, this book would never have happened.

Winthrop Academy
Foxwood Road
Cornish, Connecticut
Cornish 3-6188

1956/1957

Valued Parents,

For over a quarter century, my aim as headmistress of Winthrop Academy has been to inspire every girl to develop essential values, to awaken in her the desire to make the greatest possible use of her life, to promote sound and healthy bodies, and to maintain a challenging academic program in preparation for higher education. Our dynamic faculty, all with advanced degrees, is motivated by progressive goals and through sincere purpose has attained the highest standards of the academic world.

Winthrop Academy's philosophy is based on the values of the Christian tradition and furthers these values through everyday life. Monday through Friday, classes are held during the morning and late afternoon. Early afternoons are set aside for study hall and athletics, which include soccer, lacrosse, tennis, basketball, softball, mountain climbing and skiing. During the week, dress and structure are formal. Weekends are more relaxed with some free time to appreciate special activities in our unique country setting and climate. Three times a year we enjoy social events with our neighbor, The Bryant School for boys.

Vespers are held each evening after dinner, and Sunday services in the Winthrop Chapel, accompanied by our school choir.

The Curriculum: Classes are small, individualized, and motivational.

English and Creative Writing
Mathematics: Algebra, Geometry, Trigonometry, and Calculus
Foreign languages: Latin, French and Spanish
Sciences: Biology, Geology, Chemistry, and Physics
History: World, American, European and Asian
Creative Arts: Dramatics, Voice, Harmony, Music Composition and Theory
Art Appreciation, Studio Art, Modern Dance
Courses taught by the school Chaplain: Man and Society, Comparative Religions

Winthrop Academy is for the exceptional young lady who wishes to maximize her potential. We prepare our students for success.

Respectfully Yours,

Miss Elizabeth Hicks, Headmistress

CHAPTER ONE

January 1957

All her life Nancy had wanted to make people love her by trying to please them. Now, she felt impoverished by the nightmare of the past year and would *never* forgive her mother for her part in it. She lowered the car window and floated her arm in the air as if dipping it into a frigid mountain stream. The bright sunlight glittered on the snow-covered countryside as the brand new Lincoln Continental sped north on Route 5 along the Connecticut River. Her mother made no protest to the rush of cold air. In fact, her eyes never left the road.

If this weren't the day of "new beginnings," her mother would have lectured her about something. Anything. But of course today wasn't the right time. Her mother always waited for "right times". Mrs. Matthew Walden was known for her insistence on appropriate etiquette. Furthermore, she never made mistakes. Except for one...having Nancy. And she had suffered plenty because of it. Come to think of it, they both had. Nancy glanced down at the information that had come from the school. Her mother had placed it on Nancy's lap at the beginning of the trip and although Nancy had deliberately not touched the papers, she looked down and read the top page.

WINTHROP ACADEMY REQUIRED EQUIPMENT

Every article must be plainly marked with nametapes.

There will be a nametape inspection of clothing on the first Saturday of the school year and on the first Saturday after each vacation.

Nancy turned her eyes to the side of the road. She was glad that the last few months had been hell for her mother, too. She deserved that and so much more...a lifetime of regret. Nothing Nancy could ever do would repair the pain that lived like a constant companion in her chest. Why, her mother had demanded, couldn't Nancy be like her sister Joannie, who was excelling at college, who never gave her parents a moment's worry, who never lied, never shamed them? Nancy knew that her mother blamed her failure with Nancy on the fact that Nancy's father had traveled constantly for the last five years, leaving the burden of raising two such different girls to her. Joannie was an angel. Joannie was a success, unlike Nancy who was secretive and introverted at home. Her mother always assumed that she had nothing to offer, nothing to say, now more than ever. Mother and Joannie said it all.

WINTHROP ACADEMY REQUIRED CLOTHING

Tweed skirts and sweaters
One gray skirt
One school blazer
Four pair of silk stockings
Socks: woolen and cotton

Nancy was dying for a cigarette but smoking wasn't allowed in the car. She kicked off her brown penny loafers and slumped down, resting her head against the back of the seat. Her long dark hair framed her delicate lightly freckled face. It was early January and Connecticut had more snow than usual. Nancy liked snow when it was fresh and clean, but she knew it would lose its beauty and become dirty slush. The cold whiteness clung precariously to the barren branches as they sped past. The branches looked like a woman's arms, reaching for something that had been taken away.

"We're almost there." Mrs. Walden sounded too cheerful. Was she really that glad to see the last of her, Nancy wondered? "Would you like to stop for a bite to eat? We've obviously missed lunch at the school."

"No, we might as well get there sooner rather than later," Nancy said, sitting up to push her feet back into her shoes, deliberately pressing down on the heels.

Shoes: Oxfords or saddle shoes (moccasins are not acceptable)
Sneakers for gymnasium wear
Dress shoes with moderate heels for wear with afternoon dresses
Galoshes to fit above shoes
Eight-inch boots and cool-proof inner soles purchased from L.L Bean

Her mother usually told her to use a shoehorn. Nancy was surprised she hadn't carried one in her pocket. She wouldn't like Nancy to break down the back of her new loafers. But no comment. No such luck. *Lord, how she hated her mother.*

"Now Nancy, you should have a more positive attitude. Remember that Miss Hicks said you'll be able to make up your work quickly. With only seventy girls in Winthrop Academy, you'll get a lot of individual attention. This is an opportunity to turn over a new leaf. No one there has to know about your past."

Nancy glared at her mother. Was she making this last morale-boosting speech to assuage her conscience before she left Nancy off at school? Her mother always needed to know that she had done her duty, done the "right thing". The bonus was that soon her mother would be free of her. Nancy let the words flow past her.

"Yes, Mother. You're right, I'm going to turn over a new

leaf," Nancy said without expression, recalling how she had fought being sent away. She felt the final strain of defeat.

"Well now, you see it my way." Mrs. Walden forced a smile as she turned the car into the long driveway of the school.

Silk or wool afternoon dresses for dinner
Dresses for special occasions: one formal dress with covered shoulders and modest neckline
(Attention is called to this description)
Four cotton shirts
Two pairs dungarees
One all-wool flannel shirt
Two long leg, long sleeve union suits.
"Duo-fold" is recommended
Two aprons or smocks

Nancy scanned the campus as the car passed under a canopy of ancient elms that lined the approach to the main building. It was clearly one of those ostentatious colonial estates. To her left, neat fields stretched for miles toward rolling wooded hills. Shading her eyes, she could make out formal gardens now partially covered by snow. Stone steps led to an ornamental fountain, which no doubt sent up sparkling jets of water in the summer. There were other buildings to the right and in the distance, a large modern one featuring a good deal of glass next to an open field. She supposed it must be the gymnasium. Ski marks crisscrossed the field and up a hill to the left of the gym. Nancy shivered at the very thought.

One wool hat to be worn when outdoors from
November through March
Riding: Jodhpurs or riding breeches and riding boots
To be purchased through the school: skis,
Winthrop Academy Dark blue ski pants and parka,
cap, mitts and a lacrosse stick.

Tall clusters of frozen rhododendrons stood across from the entrance to the main building. This was going to be her life. *A new beginning.*

ADDITIONAL ARTICLES:

Bible and prayer book
Webster's Collegiate Dictionary
Flashlight
Raincoat and hat
Hot water bottle

Nancy pushed the papers from her lap onto the floor of the car. She knew she should be glad to be away from her mother, but suddenly Nancy couldn't stop herself from crying.

Sheila's Jaffrey's kinky red curls bounced as she lumbered down the full length of the narrow corridor. She liked to be the first to know about anything that happened and relished her self-imposed responsibility of informing others. The girls, scattered around the room, turned to look at her expectantly.

"What is David Brinkley's assistant about to broadcast now?" Audrey asked, flipping her dirty blonde hair out of her eyes.

Sheila made a significant -and she hoped- annoying pause before answering, because Audrey Vaughn was her favorite person. And it bugged her when she acted sarcastic and aloof.

"The new girl has arrived," she announced in an off-handed manner. "Doesn't look a bit happy about it either," she added.

"What do you mean?" Karen asked from her curled up position on the bed.

Now, Karen Phelps was different. Behind the horn-rimmed glasses, her hazel eyes were always kind. She wasn't real pretty,

Sheila thought, but she would have voted her "nicest of all" if she had had the chance.

"Well, I watched from the window when she said goodbye to her mother and it got rather emotional," Sheila said as she peeled the wrapper from a York peppermint. "As a matter of fact," she added authoritively, "the poor thing bawled her head off. Not the mother, just her."

"That's about par for what mothers want," Audrey said. "It makes them feel better. She must have done something really major to be dumped here in the middle of her senior year." Sheila had to agree. Nobody, but *nobody* came to Winthrop Academy mid year. She bet this was the first time ever.

Audrey pulled on her middle finger until it made that irritating popping sound. "What kind of car did they have?"

"Really, Audrey," Heather Brock said. "Let's give the girl a chance."

"Did I say I wouldn't?" Audrey leaned her lanky body against the wall and stuffed her hands in the pockets of her dungarees.

Sheila couldn't stand Audrey's attitude one more minute. After all, Heather was arguably the second nicest girl in the group and was always good about sharing any desserts she didn't want. Maybe Audrey was jealous of Heather's naturally curly blonde hair. Everyone was, really.

"Let's cut the crap and go downstairs," Sheila announced, raking her chubby fingers through her red curls. "Maybe we can meet her before study hall."

"What did she look like?" Heather asked as they filed out of the room.

"I couldn't see too well from the window, but she did have the school uniform on...navy blazer and gray skirt. That should impress Miss Hicks. And she has really long black hair."

Sheila heard Audrey mutter, "Who gives a damn?"

Well, Sheila thought, I do. And Audrey would too, if she'd just loosen up and let someone like her. Audrey acted like she never gave a damn about anyone and Sheila found that especially maddening since she had long tried to befriend her. Not that Audrey showed any appreciation for her efforts.

❧

Miss Elizabeth Hicks stood at her office window contemplating all she had accomplished in the past thirty years. As the granddaughter of the founder of Winthrop Academy, Miss Hicks had faithfully carried on the traditions and values established by her Grandmother Elizabeth who had retired as headmistress. Miss Hicks was only twenty-five when she took her grandmother's place.

Today, the academy not only had a reputation for the highest scholastic standing, but it was also considered the "in" preparatory school among New York and Connecticut's social elite.

Miss Hicks cherished the rambling colonial building which stood majestically in the center of the campus. She saw to it that the grounds were kept meticulously to preserve the past grandeur of the estate. The interior of the main building reflected both age and dignity with rich oriental carpets on every floor, marble fireplaces, wall tapestries, and gilt-framed paintings of her ancestors, all treasured antique furnishings handed down from past generations. And there were always fresh flowers throughout the main floor and in her suite as well.

She had never before accepted a student in the middle of the school year and now she questioned the wisdom of her decision, especially since the girl was a senior. Miss Hicks felt a deep pride in her approach to administration and believed firmly in the protocols she had established. This mid-term admission was a first for her and she had never been comfortable with firsts.

The sun glaring on the snow was so bright that it made her eyes water as she stared at the familiar grounds below. The wind had begun to pick up blowing snow in gusts across the lacrosse field creating billows that rose and swirled. Her migraine had subsided but she still felt exhausted. She massaged her temple as her thoughts continued to ramble.

Through the years, Miss Hicks observed that the more money a family had, the busier and more distracted the parents became, and the girls inevitably suffered for it. Her girls at Winthrop Academy were clear examples. When she herself had been enrolled in Winthrop Academy as a freshman, her parents had sailed for Europe the following week and she hadn't heard from them again until Thanksgiving.

Her parents had definitely not planned to have a second child, not after Paul...a fact which they didn't hesitate to make known to her. But dutifully, they had given her all the advantages of a child from a wealthy family and she had had the finest of educations, while Paul had been safely farmed out to a foster home. After their parents' untimely deaths, while she was still a student at Vassar, Miss Hicks had taken on the responsibility of her brother, keeping him safe and out of harm's way.

Miss Hicks glanced at her watch and realized she had better get ready to greet Nancy Walden. Stepping in front of the full-length Cheval mirror, she twisted around to see if the seams of her stockings were straight. She sighed at the sight of her thick, corseted torso, a result of afternoon teas with the girls and evening snacks with Sam.

Thank God she had never been a parent. It was difficult enough contending with other people's children, girls they sent away from home. They boarded their daughters in her school claiming the importance of providing them with a good education. She had never yet heard a parent admit that another reason was that they couldn't cope with them at home.

Smoothing her short wavy hair neatly behind her ears, Miss Hicks reminded herself of how desperately her girls needed affection and understanding, and she was proud of how she had provided exactly that for each one. She had a letter from a 1944 graduate who had won a Pulitzer Prize in literature, only thirteen years after she had graduated. Miss Hicks had the letter framed and it hung on the wall in such a way that visitors would be sure to see it.

Hilda Sampson, better known as Sam, interrupted her

musings by striding into the room without knocking, her leather tie pumps scuffed the pile of the Persian carpet.

"Best spruce up Beth," she said. "Our new challenge has arrived."

Miss Hicks smiled at her trusted friend and secretary, taking in her high cheek bones and a no-nonsense blunt-cut hair style that hung straight just to the bottom of her ears. Sam had been by her side from the very beginning. She loved Sam's faded blue eyes, her abrupt and straightforward manner, the way she sniffed and raised her eyebrows when something was on her mind.

"You don't think I should have accepted the Walden girl, do you?" she asked.

"What difference does it make now?" Sam said. "You seem pretty sure it'll work out putting her on the corridor with Jennifer." Miss Hicks gently placed her hand over Sam's to still her tapping fingers.

"Yes, I am," Miss Hicks replied. "Jennifer is well adjusted. I think she will be good for Nancy."

"Time will tell," Sam said in at tone that Miss Hicks knew only too well.

Nancy balanced the teacup on her knees as she observed Miss Hicks' sitting room. It was like a museum, she noted, impressed by the magnificent furnishings. She couldn't believe she was here. Any courage she had mustered for this first meeting unraveled like a row of stitches. *Why, why had her mother forced her to come to this place?* How could she face all these people and act like nothing had happened? She was a husk; she had never been so empty.

She accepted a cookie from the plate passed to her by Jennifer Stewart, her new roommate. Jennifer was pretty with her shiny brown hair in a perfect pageboy that just brushed the neck of her pastel blue cashmere twin set. Her pearls hung just below the neckline. She seemed friendly, but Nancy hadn't wanted a roommate. She had warned her mother about that only to be told that it wouldn't be good for her to spend a lot of time alone.

"...and so you'll be under Jennifer's wing."

Lost in thought as she had been, Nancy was startled by Miss Hicks' voice. "Pardon me?"

"I said, my dear, that I shall place you under Jennifer's wing for the remainder of the afternoon. She can acquaint you with the buildings and introduce you to the other students. First, however, I suggest you get yourself unpacked."

When Sam placed her teacup on an ornate oval tray, Nancy was reminded that her mother used her sterling only for special occasions. She blinked her eyes, blanking out any thoughts of home.

Miss Hicks acts nice enough, she thought, but if she tells, Lord, if she tells anyone, I'll run away. Disappear forever.

"Jennifer dear, be sure to show Nancy where my office is located. Nancy, if you have any questions or problems, that is where to find me."

"I'll be glad to." Standing up, Jennifer smiled at Miss Hicks, smoothing her tight skirt down over her hips. Nancy observed that her roommate appeared taller than she actually was because of her erect posture.

"My luggage..." Nancy began as she and Jennifer left the sitting room.

"The Creep took care if it," Jennifer said and waved her hand in the air as if some type of magic had occurred. "Here it is."

"The Creep?"

Jennifer laughed. "Our grotesque janitor, Mr. Jones, alias "The Creep". He's always lurking, and he sweats so much you can't miss him. But he's harmless."

"Oh." There was something about the relish with which Jennifer described him that Nancy found repellent. Surely the man couldn't be as revolting as she made him out to be. "I'll have to thank him."

"Don't bother. He hasn't spoken more than three words to any girl in the century he's been here."

"Boy, he sounds really eccentric," Nancy said.

"You know it."

The two girls, laden with Nancy's belongings, paused on the stairs to let a group of students pass.

"Well, Nancy, you may as well meet the gang who live in the annex with us," Jennifer said. "We call it "The Corridor" and it only has room for six outstanding seniors. All the other poor slobs live in separate residential buildings and have to walk up here for meals and classes. Ladies, this is Nancy Walden."

Jennifer began to make the introductions as if she was queen of Winthrop Academy and the girls surrounding Nancy were her subjects. She proceeded to make such sharp-tongued introductions that Nancy felt uneasy.

"Sheila Jaffrey, room next to ours. Harmless except that she eats and talks too much."

Flushing, Sheila jammed a candy wrapper into her jacket pocket as if it were burning her hand.

"Heather Brock's in the room across the hall from us," Jennifer continued. "She's our Mother Protector. You can count on her to stick up for the underdog." Heather was short and busty, with curly blonde hair and sad blue eyes. She had a friendly smile but Nancy sensed that it hid embarrassment.

"Karen Phelps. Likes to please. Everyone's pal and head of the student council." It was clear from Jennifer's tone of voice that Karen had not quite made it to best friend status. As she said hello, she tugged on her over-sized sweatshirt which had the Boston Red Sox written across its front with Ted Williams' number nine below. Some boy's, no doubt. Well, she certainly was the thinnest of the girls. Maybe, Nancy thought, that bothered Jennifer.

"And last but not least, Audrey Vaughn," Jennifer announced a little too loudly. "Don't argue with her. She knows it all and isn't afraid to tell you." Audrey was tall with a Dutch Boy haircut. Nancy saw the two girls lock glances as if they knew each other's strengths and weaknesses precisely. Audrey turned and bolted down the stairs, taking them two at a time.

"Don't mind her, she's self-conscious," Shelia said. "Come on, you guys, we've got to bug out or we'll be late to study hall. See you later, Nancy."

Sheila was certainly the peacemaker in the group. Nancy could see that right away.

"Glad to meet all of you." Nancy called to their receding backs. Overwhelmed by the events of the day thus far, Nancy found herself wondering how Jennifer would have characterized her had she been on the receiving end of one of those cryptic introductions. She was not certain that she ever wanted to know.

"Nobody cares what I say," Jennifer explained as though reading her mind. "After you live so close together for half a year, you get to know each other pretty damn well. You'll find out. By the way, that door we just passed at the head of the stairs is Miss Hicks' office. That's where you want to be sure *not* to go if you have a problem. She's so psyched up herself that I doubt if she could help anyone find their way out of a paper bag. Wait till you hear her '*words to live by*'."

Nancy wondered if Jennifer saw everything as something to scoff at. Why did she seem so bitter? And what will she be like to actually room with?

"Anyway," Jennifer continued, "next to her is Miss Sampson's office, and next to that is the infirmary. Sam kinda doubles as secretary and nurse and buddy to Miss Hicks. They make quite a team, if that's what you want to call it. Some people might call it something else." Jennifer raised her eyebrows in an exaggerated expression and seemed to be insinuating something, but Nancy was not sure what. Whatever it was, it was bound to be something unpleasant.

"And over there is where our mail boxes are," Jennifer said as she pointed to the far end of the large space just beyond the stairs leading down to the reception hall. "It's a popular place to hang out every day after lunch if you have someone who remembers you're here."

Nancy figured she might as well skip that daily activity.

The girls struggled on with Nancy's suitcases as they started down a long narrow corridor which was clearly part of the annex that jutted out of the north side of the main building. "Here's home sweet home," Jennifer told her.

Nancy entered the room behind Jennifer and set her bags down in the middle of the floor. With the exception of a few personal things on Jennifer's bureau and a signed photograph of Elvis Presley on her bulletin board, she saw little evidence that anyone lived here. Nancy couldn't tell if all the rooms were kept like this or if Jennifer was just a neat-nik.

There were two of everything: beds, desks, chair, mirrors, bureaus, lamps, and closets. The walls were a pale green and there were white curtains at the windows. The matching bedspreads, beige, with Kelly green scrolls, provided the only splash of color. The bulletin board over Nancy's desk was bare, waiting for Nancy to enhance it...as if she had any happy memories to stick up there.

"This is your new home," Jennifer said cheerfully. "Count your blessings; it's the only double room on the corridor. You should see the size of the single rooms if you think this is bad."

While Nancy unpacked, Jennifer primped in front of the mirror and talked non-stop about the faculty, school routines, her likes and dislikes. She had, Nancy discovered, opinions about everything. And she appeared to be totally unselfconscious. "I think I'll change into a turtleneck for dinner," Jennifer said, half to herself. She stripped off her sweater and Nancy saw that she wore no bra underneath.

"They're small, but they stick right out there," Jennifer said as Nancy averted her eyes. Jennifer was actually flaunting herself, admiring her own breasts in the mirror. "I never wear a bra. I've heard that they break down your muscles. Besides, men don't like them."

Jennifer pulled a soft green sweater over her head. It was tight. Not enough to flatten her but enough so you couldn't miss what was there. "By the way, don't leave your undies around. They seem to disappear into thin air."

Lord, I'm rooming with a weirdo. Does she mean that she takes other people's underwear? Looking for a distraction, Nancy pulled out the drawers of her bureau and rearranged the clothes she had just put in there. Jennifer didn't even notice.

Jennifer curled her eyelashes, admiring the result in her mirror. "There are three male teachers," she continued, "and they all live in faculty cottages on the school grounds. Mr. and Mrs. Burroughs, both teach science; they're older and real intellectuals. Then, there is Mr. Packer who teaches philosophy and art. His wife Andrea just had a baby. They're young and friendly but..."

Nancy interrupted, "What did she have?"

"I don't know. A girl, I think. Anyway, with two being married, you can imagine which one of the three I have my eye on; Mr. Jonathan Herrick is our teacher of English and the object of my attention. I'm prepared for anything."

Nancy chose not to respond. Her roommate was obviously boy crazy and to think that she was going to have to live with this for the next five months.

"Oh God, look at the clock," Jennifer exclaimed. "I'll tell you more tonight, but now we've got to get downstairs for dinner. If there's anything you have to be around here, it's prompt. That's one of Miss Hicks' favorite words." Jennifer explained over her shoulder that Miss Hicks had a saying to go with anything that was fun or fattening. As Nancy hurried close behind Jennifer, she felt somehow as though she'd been caught up in a whirlwind not of her choice.

In the dining room, there were ten round tables covered with white linen tablecloths. The linen napkins held in individual rings were replaced every day, Jennifer told Nancy. She added that each girl was assigned to a certain table for one week at a time with a teacher presiding, including one table where no one could speak anything but French. She said that was a blast since French was one of her favorite subjects.

Nancy was assigned to sit with Jennifer at Miss Hicks' table. They stood behind their chairs waiting for the signal of grace. Nancy had started to seat herself but swiftly rose again, horrified. *Bless this food to our lips and us to Thy loving service...* A loud "amen" resounded across the dining room as the girls pulled out their chairs and sat down.

Throughout the meal, except when answering direct questions, Nancy kept her eyes riveted on her watch. *This must be the longest day of my life.*

❧

Back in the corridor, Nancy learned from Karen that student smoking had been completely forbidden until two years ago. Now, it was a limited privilege at specific hours of the day, only in the student lounges, one of which was on their corridor.

"Good Lord, I'd die of a nicotine fit if we couldn't smoke at all," Nancy said.

Abuse of this privilege, she was told, would result in immediate suspension because Miss Hicks really didn't want anyone to smoke in the first place, even outdoors. It was beginning to be very clear that a rule was a rule here at Winthrop as long as Miss Hicks was around to enforce it.

"Hell, we're so glad to be able to smoke now that no one dares to break the rules," Karen told her. "Besides, we would never get away with it. Miss Wade, the history teacher and our house mother here on our corridor, patrols our hallway every night after the lights-out bell rings...until the last one of us is asleep."

Nancy turned to Jennifer, and asked which one was Miss Wade.

"She's the one with the pretty face and the piano legs. That's a point in our favor though. You usually have time to douse the light 'cause you can hear her heavy stockings rubbing together long before she gets to your door. We call her "Waddles." She seems sweet, but watch out because she's a religious fanatic underneath."

Everyone snickered when Sheila stood up and did an exaggerated, knees-together walk with her palms pressed together as though praying and her eyes rolled heavenward.

"While we're on the subject, I did smell smoke when I opened my window the other night. It was coming from your room, Audrey."

Nancy's heart skipped a beat when she saw the look Audrey gave Jennifer.

"Piss on you, Jennifer. That's a lie."

"Hey, I was only kidding. Besides, your family has so much money, 'ol Hicks would never kick you out."

"Mind your effing business." Audrey jumped to her feet. It was the third time in twenty minutes that Nancy had seen her crack her knuckles.

"Miss Wade's not that bad, Jennifer," Heather scolded. "You're going to give Nancy the wrong picture of this place before she has a chance to make her own observations." It was evident to Nancy that Heather was trying to change the subject.

"Yeah," Sheila chimed in. "Anyone feel like some treats before the lights-out bell?" She looked around the room. "For Pete's sake, you'd think I'm the only one around here whose got a sweet tooth."

"You're also the only one, Sheila, who has put on about forty pounds since September," Audrey snapped. She was sorry the minute she said it. Nancy could see that. It seemed like Sheila was the only person who treated Audrey like a human being.

"Thanks a bunch, Audrey," Sheila muttered. "Well, goodnight, Nancy. It's great to have you aboard." She slammed the door behind her as she left the room. Everyone was aware that Sheila felt hurt.

"Don't worry," Jennifer said. "She won't starve. She has a drawer full of goodies in her room."

"Well folks, guess I'll grab a quick shower," Karen said, stretching. A chorus of goodnights followed her out the door.

The warning bell rang at twenty minutes past nine, giving the girls ten minutes to get in bed with their lights out. Heather and Audrey left the room at the same time, Heather said good night, but Audrey simply walked out with long angry strides.

How different they were, Nancy thought. She sensed loneliness in all of them. Perhaps she was just transposing her own feelings of abandonment and emptiness, but it seemed there was something that bound the girls together. She wondered what it would be like to have a real friend, a best friend.

When Jennifer started to undress, Nancy, embarrassed, took her pajamas and walked down to the bathroom to change in a tiny, but at least private, toilet stall. By the time she returned to her room, she found to her relief that Jennifer was in bed with her light out. Turning out her own bedside lamp, Nancy crawled into bed and relaxed for the first time since she had arrived.

Under the covers, Jennifer cupped her breast and thought of Mr. Herrick. She'd get him one day, she told herself, tease him out of his mind until he was begging for her body. And then maybe, just maybe, she'd give herself to him. Her nipples were hard under her hands as her mind wandered. The sensation sent a thrill of anticipation through her body. Jennifer turned onto her side, tried to see that petite pony-tailed girl in the bed across the room. There was something mysterious about her. She was too serious. Far too serious for Jennifer's taste, at least.

CHAPTER TWO

The first week was over, and somehow Nancy had managed to get through those first few days without forgetting too many names, being late too many times, or attending too many wrong classes. She was grateful that she had been so busy that there was little time to dwell on her own problems. Now that Friday had arrived however, it was a letdown rather than a relief. At least during the week each moment of the day was scheduled. Karen said that weekends were great because they gave you more free time. Nancy was not looking forward to that since whatever she was doing, sitting in the smoking lounge or writing a paper, was overlaid with something she had done two years before. This was whether it was fooling around with Philip, arguing with her mother, or watching her sister play basketball with her father one brilliant fall afternoon in the driveway of her house in Scarsdale.

Each morning, when she heard the bell sound off in the corridor, she was both rising out of bed to dress for breakfast downstairs and rushing out the door at home to catch the bus for high school. In the shadows of the room, she could see the girl she had once been, flicking her long black hair over her shoulders, waiting for time to pass so she could grow up. Then there was last year, when her life as she knew it had imploded. How she wished she had been stronger. Now she'd have to act as if it all made sense, day after day, but she would always be lonely, always pretending.

Lights out was at ten on weekends. Big deal, Nancy thought. She had been used to reading late into the night over the last year with no one to bother her. For no reason, she pictured the warped full-length mirror in her bathroom at home and how she used to think it distorted her reflection. Now, however, she knew that what she had seen there was true.

It must have been eleven-thirty when Jennifer whispered, "Nancy, are you awake?"

"Yes," Nancy said, reluctant to answer. She really did not want to enter into any discussion with Jennifer especially when she was not the one choosing the subject.

"Oh, good. I just can't get to sleep. It's so damn dull around here. There's nothing to do but eat and sleep, sleep and eat. Christ, a person could go buggy. What do you think of Jonathan?"

"Who?"

"You know, Mr. Herrick."

"Oh, yes. Well, he's okay I guess."

"Okay? Jesus, you are out to lunch. He's the only available pair of pants around here, that's all. Did you notice the look on his face when I came into class this morning? I swear he got a hard-on right there in class...Nancy, you still awake?"

Astounded by such talk, Nancy closed her eyes hoping to fall asleep. Yes, she was there, she indicated with an elaborate yawn. She had never really talked to anyone about boys, certainly not her mother and after what happened to her, forever would be soon enough.

"Remember," Jennifer continued, "I told you I won't have a worry in the world when my moment with Jonathan arrives? The truth is I have enough contraceptive pills to supply the entire school with six months of orgies. Isn't that the cat's meow?"

"What are you talking about? What kind of pills?"

"My father is a gynecologist and a salesman gave him a ton of samples of this new kind of pill that's not even on the market yet. Doctor Daddy said that they developed it for cramps when you have the curse, but the tests indicate that it works as birth control. All you have to do is just take a pill a day and you won't get pregnant. How good is that?"

Nancy muffled an involuntary exclamation. Her head was spinning with confusion and fatigue. Jennifer droned on.

"Good old Doctor Daddy," Jennifer continued, "so busy being a wonderful doctor...too busy to pay attention to me. And then there's Mumsie, the pillar of the community, on every committee, on all the sucker lists. Including mine. I was going with Gerard, and one fine day I announced to the home front that I might be pregnant."

This time Nancy gasped aloud, dismayed by the thought that Jennifer might have had a baby. She opened her eyes, wide awake now, anxious for her to go on.

"Shocked you didn't I?" Jennifer said gleefully. "You can imagine how my parents reacted. And they're supposed to be two intelligent people. Jesus, it was such a joke that I could hardly keep from laughing in their faces. You know why? 'Cause at that point in my life, I had never even seen a *dinkus*. But I must admit I was getting damn curious."

Nancy couldn't believe her ears.

Had Jennifer actually thought she was being funny? She forced herself to remain silent, hoping that Jennifer would come to the end of her story soon. It was more difficult than Nancy could have guessed; to have to listen to someone who came close to an experience as dreadful as hers had been and yet could tell about it so flippantly. She could not, and she would not ever talk about what happened to her. Ever.

"Well, I could take the tears and recriminations for about two days and that was it," Jennifer continued. "Then I told them I got the curse. Mumsie didn't believe me. Do you know I actually had to show her proof? But, needless to say, my point was made. Doctor Daddy took me into his office, gave me a talk about the birds and bees. Then my mother came in to explain how she and Doctor Daddy are progressive parents. So, to make a long story short, I left the office with those soul-freeing little pills. Mission accomplished."

"Parents are really something, you know?" Jennifer announced. "They don't really care what the hell you do as long as there won't be consequences that would hurt their precious reputations."

Nancy had to agree with that statement, but that was all she agreed with. Getting out of bed, she stumbled toward the door. Her bare feet slapped on the wooden floor as she ran down the hall to the bathroom. It was going to be a long night since she would not return to her room until she was certain Jennifer was asleep. Jennifer was an enigma. Imagine lying to your parents like that. Nancy had always been taught by word and example not to talk about intimate things like secret yearnings or anger or especially, sex. Now she couldn't seem to shut Jennifer's words out of her mind.

Saturday, and finally some free time. Nancy bundled up and hurried down the back stairs, not wanting to see anyone. Leaving the parking lot at the back of the main building, she wended her way past a row of barren elm trees and across the snow-covered soccer field. She climbed a slight rise from which she could look down at the academy. It was so cold that she shifted her weight from one foot to the other. She would have given a lot for a cigarette but there were those rules that could not be broken. Defiantly, she took out a Kool and put it unlit between her lips. It made her feel in control somehow, and that was something she badly needed at this point. She wondered if the teachers spent their weekends patrolling the grounds hoping to catch a student breaking some rule or other.

It was possible that someone was spying from a window right now, waiting to see if she would light this cigarette, but she didn't care. She had already broken one of life's major rules. How would one more matter?

Nancy had spent almost an hour the previous night in the small but safe toilet stall waiting for Jennifer to fall asleep. She was too frightened of what she might do or say if she had to listen to any more details about her roommate's sex life. That morning Jennifer gave her a puzzled, almost innocent look, which aggravated Nancy even more. Nothing further had been said.

Nancy shuddered. She could not bear to stay in that room,

silent, listening to Jennifer as though she approved. At least she had been in love with Philip, no matter how much her mother had tried to prove that she hadn't. Nancy hated herself for being no better than Jennifer.

After trudging through the woods a bit further, she brushed the snow off a large rock and sat down. The unlit cigarette was still dangling from her mouth. Memories of the past year surfaced relentlessly. She closed her eyes and remembered in vivid detail the morning she had told her mother.

"Pregnant?" Her mother had hissed in an ominously quiet voice.

"Oh, Mother, it isn't so bad, really," she had replied. "I'll be almost eighteen by the time the baby is born. Philip and I are in love. We can get married quickly and quietly so no one will ever have to...."

"PREGNANT!" Mrs. Walden interrupted her. "My daughter is pregnant, for God and the whole world to see? All that boy wanted from you was sex, you stupid girl. He doesn't love you. When did it happen? Was it when you said you were at Cheryl's house for a sleep over? Oh God, what will everyone say?"

Nancy's brown eyes were glazed with fear. "Don't make it into something dirty," Nancy begged her. "Please stop screaming."

"Stop screaming?" her mother shrieked, "how dare you say that to me, you little—you little whore."

Right then, her mother had slapped her across the face, not once, but repeatedly, all the time saying, "Joannie would never shame me like this."

Nancy had clenched her hands and dug her nails into her palms. Tears stung her cheeks as she stood there holding her breath. Her mother's voice had dropped to a frightening, hoarse whisper. "Oh God...how could you do this to me?"

Nancy was too shocked at her mother's violent reaction to feel anything other than terror when her mother's eyes bulged and her face turned ashen except for dark red blotches high on each cheek. Nancy watched her as though in a trance.

Everything seemed to happen in slow motion. Her mother's hands began to shake uncontrollably and she stood sobbing in the middle of the room. Nancy had frozen when her mother fell to the floor.

"Oh Mother, I'm sorry," she had said. "Please be all right. I'll do anything. I'm sorry. I'm so, so sorry."

That, Nancy reflected, had been her undoing. Once again, her mother had instinctively done and said the right thing at the right time, bending Nancy to her will. Why couldn't her mother have listened to ***her*** for a change? Really listened. After all, she had never told Joannie what to do and how to do it. Nancy squeezed her eyes closed, desperate to hold back the tears. She felt so empty. Her mother was right. She was of no consequence. A numbing shame and guilt so familiar to her now seemed to settle over everything.

When Nancy had been able to sneak a call to Philip, he had agreed all too quickly that maybe her mother was right. He was obviously relieved to be free of the whole idea of a baby, free to go to Yale like his father.

So, of course there had been no wedding. Her mother had announced that Nancy would go to the Florence Crittendon House for unwed mothers in Boston. No daughter of Mrs. Matthew Walden would be married under such despicable circumstances. And she didn't want to hear about love. It had been nothing but sex, something that good Christian married couples avoid until they wished to plan a family. Why couldn't Nancy admit that, at least?

Her mother's words had shamed her to the very marrow. If she had stripped her naked and beaten her, Nancy could not have felt more humiliated. Never, never could things be the same. Never again would she believe in herself. She had wept profusely for something gone forever.

Nancy picked up some snow and kept packing it between her mittens until it became an ice ball. She threw it as hard as she could at a birch tree and missed. Now, less than a year later, it was over and done with. Except that it wasn't. She had changed physically...not really a girl any more. With her breasts that had been so full and heavy with milk only a month ago, and the ugly stretch marks remaining on her stomach, Nancy felt different.

At the end of her sixth month, she had no longer been able to hide what was happening to her body, and Nancy's mother had announced that they would leave for Boston that weekend. Daylight came and she had dressed herself slowly and miserably. Her head ached and the toast stuck in her throat. How was she ever going to get through the agony of the next three months? She had wept then, begging her mother not to force her to go. That was the time when her everyday world moved away in an arc far from her senior prom and college visits, separating her from her past with brutal indifference.

And now her baby belonged to someone else, for God's sake. It had been a girl. They had told her that, at least. But she would never know where she was, or if the people who had adopted her were good parents. It was painful to remember how easily she had given in to her parents' demands.

Nancy didn't hear the sound of footsteps in the powdery snow. "My dear, my dear, what are we doing?" Miss Wade said, as she plodded along, trying to keep snow from getting in her boots.

Taken completely by surprise, Nancy's mouth dropped open and the forgotten cigarette stuck precariously to her lower lip.

"Wet your lips," Miss Wade ordered, cupping her hand expectantly under the dangling cigarette.

Staring into Miss Wade's hazel eyes, Nancy spit it out.

It occurred to Nancy that Miss Wade was pretty, particularly now with her cheeks pink with cold, and her dark hair curled softly around the edges of her white angora hat.

"My dear, what are we doing?" she repeated. The cigarette rested in her hand like prime evidence in a trial.

Suddenly, anxious for Miss Wade to believe that she was not breaking a rule, Nancy began turning her pockets inside out.

"Honestly, Miss Wade, I wasn't planning on smoking it. I was just holding it in my mouth. See? I don't even have any matches. It's just a habit. I used to smoke so much. But I swear, I swear to God, I wasn't going to light it."

Out of breath, Nancy stopped, surprised at her own outburst. She took a deep breath and held it as she watched Miss Wade slowly, deliberately, crumble the cigarette in her hand. Her heavy coat billowed out as she bent to bury it in the snow.

"We must not use God to back up our frailties, my dear. We must prostrate ourselves before Him. Never use His name in that way again. Now come along."

The two walked in silence, one with her head held high as if communing with God, and one with face almost hidden by her long dark hair, both deep in thought.

"After reading your records and observing you this past week, I feel that I know what your problem is, Nancy," Miss Wade said finally. "You have lost God."

Nancy could not believe her ears. God? What was this woman doing talking to her about God? Nancy kept her eyes down, watching their feet move in unison along the road leading back to the school.

"It won't be easy for you, my dear, for you have sinned and God will punish you. But if you damn yourself and beg His forgiveness, He will eventually allow you within His grace once more."

She knows. Lord, she knows! Was nothing sacred? Nancy crossed her arms on her chest and squeezed hard, determined not to lose control. What she would like to do is to tell her to mind her own damn business, to ask her if she could imagine the pain of carrying a baby for nine months and then have it taken away. Against your will. Where was her God then?

"You have given your body once, and that was evil," Miss Wade continued briskly. Now you must give your whole self, body and soul, to God. When you have done that completely and unselfishly, you will have found Him," Miss Wade concluded on a triumphal note.

So, she couldn't trust Miss Hicks. Her mother had assured her that she had been sworn to complete confidence about the reason for Nancy's transfer. Would Miss Wade tell anyo *could she ever trust?*

When they reached the entrance of the school, Miss touched Nancy's cheek with her gloved hand. "Now run along my dear and we'll forget about what happened in the woods. Let's just dwell on these thoughts we've shared today, shall we? We'll have another talk again soon."

"Thank you, Miss Wade," Nancy said, "you're so understanding. I'll try hard to be like you."

Lord, she would never want to be like that crazy spinster. What could she know about love? In the last year, Nancy had learned more about loss than her mother and Miss Wade together knew in their lifetimes. There was no benevolent God to help her. She could just die right there in the driveway, she thought, as she headed for the back door of the annex. No one could make her pain or this feeling of emptiness go away. Not God and certainly not Miss Wade.

Nancy sat idly in the late afternoon study hall. It was a large impersonal room filled with girls fidgeting at desks and a teacher glaring at them from the front of the room. Often, another teacher patrolled the back. This torture went on from three forty-five to five-thirty, five afternoons a week with another session from seven to eight-thirty. Even if you had completed your homework, you had to sit there and appear busy. Some girls covered certain novels with brown paper to read in study hall, praying to not be caught. *Lady Chatterley's Lover* and *Lolita* were current favorites but it would be too risky to bring in a *True Confessions* which could usually be found stored away in a ski boot or a sanitary napkin box in a bedroom closet. To quote Miss Hicks: "If a student didn't learn anything, it certainly wasn't the faculty's fault."

The past few weeks had been a nightmare. *Those awful ski lessons.* All sports were required whether you liked it or not. Three times last week they had climbed up the slippery hill to stand freezing to death as they waited for their turn to make a fool of themselves with that Swiss ski instructor screaming at them to "bend zee knees."

Like a fugitive, Nancy had fled from one activity to another, frantically avoiding Miss Wade during the day and dreading nights when she had no choice but to be alone with Jennifer.

Somehow, Nancy came to associate the loss of her baby with Jennifer. She picked up a Physics book, opening it at random. What Miss Wade had said about God punishing her haunted her because she knew that her punishment wasn't for *having* a baby, but for deserting her. God had probably sent Jennifer as a curse, and now she was supposed to reform her roommate as penance. Ha! Maybe there was some truth in Miss Wade's fanatical ideas. Nancy glanced around and caught sight of Jennifer just as she left the study hall.

Mr. Herrick was the teacher on study hall duty today. Above his desk was a huge poster of Sputnik that had been launched recently by the Soviets. Nancy observed him over the top of her book. He was tall and thin but with broad shoulders, a high forehead and dark wavy hair combed straight back. Behind his horn-rimmed glasses, his eyes were a clear blue, hooded by thick eyebrows. This look might appeal to Jennifer, but it definitely did not to Nancy. She watched as her roommate returned from the bathroom and deliberately sauntered in front of Mr. Herrick, swinging her hips rhythmically in a skirt that couldn't fit any tighter, as she sashayed back to her desk.

As for Mr. Herrick, his eyes were glued to Jennifer's swaying backside, his lips slack with concentration. *How disgusting could anyone get?* Nancy thought. It was too bad he couldn't just hop aboard that satellite and disappear into space. Then perhaps she wouldn't have to listen to Jennifer ramble on about him anymore.

The bell rang. There was a sudden rustle of papers and thumping of books as they were put away now that the enforced silence was broken. Nancy joined the swarm of chattering girls as they burst from the room. Mr. Jones, The Creep, shuffled into the study hall with a push broom in hand and began cleaning up the debris. Nancy had never really seen his face since he wouldn't look up from the floor when the girls were around, but the bright florescent lights made his bald head glisten like a newly waxed floor. He shoved chairs and desks aside, his way of complaining about their thoughtlessness.

There was something menacing in his very silence, as if he had been boiled down into that lumpy body until all that remained was this concentrated bit of quiet mystery. Why do they have someone like that working here? He frightened her.

"We must respect Mr. Jones," Miss Hicks had told Nancy. "We are lucky to have such a loyal and patient helper in our school family."

After study hall, most of the girls rushed hopefully toward their mailboxes. Everyone had to look, although they knew most of the boxes would be empty. They all wanted mail, but few received it. Thus, mail time created a certain bond between them. Usually the ones who got a letter would share their news by reading it aloud to her friends.

"We eat again, ladies," Sheila shouted good-naturedly, kneeling heavily on the floor to open her laundry case.

"Just like clockwork," Audrey sneered. Every Friday, Sheila Jaffrey received clean laundry back from her mother; the case actually filled more with things to eat than to wear. She didn't seem to care that everyone knew she would rather have food than clean clothes. Watching Sheila over the top of her own letter, Audrey knew there would be another newsy epistle from that happy family of hers.

Sheila tried to catch someone's eye so that she could read her letter out loud. She would, she thought, try Audrey who was just now taking an envelope out of her box. Sheila knew it would contain the monthly check as usual. Audrey was always bitchy afterward. Sheila determined to cheer her up.

Audrey saw Sheila moving her way with her laundry case

in tow and waving a letter. *Oh Christ, here comes that big fat lapdog with another one of her family scriptures.* She couldn't take listening to one more happy, happy note from home which appeared to be like heaven on earth. If that was the case, why was Sheila stuck off in this dump with the rest of us?

Leaning against the wall, Audrey quickly read through the brief letter from her father's attorney. He always enclosed a cheerful little note assuring her how much Mr. Vaughan and the former Mrs. Vaughan missed their daughter. Why the hell didn't he forego the lies and just send the check? *Who needed that love and miss-you shit?* If her, pardon-the-expression, parents, wanted her to know something, she was sure they'd contact Hicks who in turn, would inform her...through the proper channels, of course. And if that weren't enough, here came Sheila lumbering toward her. That girl was too dumb to know when she's not wanted. Kick her in the teeth and she'd be back for more the next day. How thick can anyone be?

Folding her check into a small square, Audrey tucked it inside her bra. Then she deliberately tore up the lawyer's letter, making sure that Sheila noticed. Throwing the scraps in the wastebasket, she prepared to listen to whatever Sheila wanted to read to her. It was, she thought, the price she paid for keeping her affairs to herself.

Heather hesitated before looking in her mailbox, hardly daring to hope for a letter from her father. The new Mrs. Brock, who to Heather would always be Mrs. Eleanor Yeager the-family-busting-bitch, wrote regularly in a glowing, friendly, heartwarming manner, urging Heather to be happy, work hard, and write once in a while because "We miss you so much."

"We." Oh God, what unadulterated bull! Heather inhaled deeply and turned to look squarely into her mailbox. Nothing. Well, what did she expect? She turned away smiling at the middle distance as she skirted the groups of girls on her way to dinner. It was, she knew, important to always be on time, to make a good show.

There was the exception to every rule. Karen Phelps never failed to find at least one letter waiting for her. She was attending Winthrop Academy because of its high academic standards, not as an escape from a dysfunctional family situation. Each of her parents, plus her two brothers, wrote often and always included the most recent *Life Magazine* to keep her up on current events.

"Hi Nancy," said Jennifer pushing past her roommate to reach into her box. "Well, imagine that, it's empty. My fan mail must have been delayed." She patted the back of her pageboy. "Well, gotta' go spruce up. I've got a hot appointment with you-know-who right after dinner. I need some extra help."

Winking at Nancy she laughed as she ran down the hall to their room.

She needed help, all right, Nancy thought bitterly, help that would involve something more than simply sprucing up.

But she forgot her roommate when she saw a letter in her box. Maybe it was from Philip. Or the adoption agency. But what was she thinking? *Lord, she must be crazy*. She hadn't seen or heard from Philip for almost a year and her mother had made her sign the release papers for her baby guaranteeing that she would never see her. Never.

It was, Nancy knew, ridiculous that a simple letter could upset her so she put it in her pocket, deliberately not looking at it. But for the first time since she had come here, she hurried down the winding stairs to dinner.

Nancy was just ending a week of torture at Miss Wade's table. Lord, if she had to listen to one more lecture on how to find God, she thought she'd jump out of her skin. Two nights ago, Miss Wade had cornered her after evening study hall, the only free time of the day and she had invited Nancy into her private sitting room for another "little chat" on her spiritual progress. It appeared that for some reason she had been singled out for special attention although it didn't seem to matter to the teacher that Nancy was not responding to her passion.

Nancy swallowed a small creamed onion, whole. 'One must always eat whatever is served; something of everything,' was one of Miss Hicks' adages to live by, a part of developing self-discipline and social graces. Nancy looked doubtfully at the remaining onion on her plate in a small puddle of watery cream sauce, resolving to spit this one into her napkin. Funny, but it was more important to have a letter than to read it. She certainly couldn't read it until after study hall, because if she was caught in the act, the letter would be confiscated. This was another of Miss Hicks' ridiculous rules.

Idly fingering the scalloped edge of the tablecloth, Nancy focused on the conversation at the table. "I didn't even sign up," Sheila was saying as she reached for the serving bowl of creamed onions.

"Do you want some more, Nancy?" she asked. "They're really good."

"No thank you," Nancy said. "I'm full."

Miss Wade picked up her knife and gently tapped the table for attention. "When ladies at Winthrop Academy are asked if they would care for another serving, the answer must be; 'No thank you, I've had a gentle sufficiency.' I'm surprised you didn't learn that at Miss Hicks' table last week, Nancy."

While Miss Wade spoke, Sheila served herself the remains, scraping the bowl thoroughly.

"I hate dances." Sheila continued.

"It is your duty to join in these social functions, girls," Miss Wade lectured as she glanced around the table, "after all, they are planned for your specific pleasure and this is the last one of the year. You know that Miss Hicks considers your attendance a display of school spirit, and although it is not a requirement, it is noticed by the office if you don't go."

Though her tone was pleasant, Nancy felt the threat that hung in the air. Thankful for the distraction, she watched a scholarship student clear the table, envying her for not having to sit at the table and listen to this nonsense.

Sheila broke the silence. "Well, of course I hadn't thought of it in that sense, 'cause I do have loads of school spirit and all. It's just that most of the boys are smaller than I am and they make me feel so gross."

Her friends protested.

"They do," Sheila affirmed loudly. "You know it, and I know it."

Miss Wade cleared her throat authoritatively. "No one is perfect, but we must make the best of what we have. You're face is very pretty, Sheila, and you have lovely curly hair."

Lord, Nancy thought when she saw Miss Wade's far away expression, it's as though she were talking about herself. How pathetic can you get?

"But your enthusiasm is most advantageous my dear," Miss Wade continued. "Personality is nine-tenths of popularity. When one is at peace with God..."

Miss Wade was interrupted when Miss Hicks signaled for everyone in the dining hall to stand and prepare to leave the room.

The girls filed out, spines straight, hands at their sides. Until, that is, they entered the reception hall where during the next fifteen to twenty minutes before evening study period, most of them stood talking in small groups, their voices picking up momentum. Some girls went to the library for reference books, while a few planned conferences with teachers on subjects in which they needed extra help.

Nancy saw Jennifer hurry toward Mr. Herrick's homeroom. Extra help, she knew, was the last thing on Jennifer's mind.

Nancy was still trying to decide whether or not she should

read her letter in the next few minutes when Sheila grabbed her arm and pulled her into a cluster of chattering girls.

"Wow, did I put my foot right into it," Sheila told them. "Didn't I, Nancy? Old Waddles sure climbed on my back about that stupid dance. Now I suppose I'll have to go."

"'If you don't sign up for the dance, you don't have school spirit.' That's according to Miss Wade," Sheila mimicked. "And those who do not have school spirit will not be smiled upon by God." Their laughter was muted as they glanced about to be certain that no adult was within earshot.

"That's not exactly the way she put it," Nancy interjected, trying to be fair, but no one listened. It was, she knew, more fun to ridicule anything or anyone in authority.

Each label amused them more than the next: "Waddles. The Morals-Monger. Demented. Unbalanced. Frustrated nun. Fanatic." This was clearly one of their favorite forms of entertainment. In fact, your cleverness seemed to be measured by the sharpness of your tongue. How was she ever going to fit in here?

It seemed to her that the only way to prove your worth in this group was to slander someone or other, even though Nancy had to admit that in Miss Wade's case, she sure was stuck on religion. Nancy slipped away from the group unnoticed. She intended to go to the library to read her letter. Just then, the study hall bell rang.

Jennifer, her sweater tight over her breasts, knocked gently on the door to Mr. Herrick's office and walked confidently into the room, closing the door firmly behind her. He sat at his desk, reading as usual, wearing the prescribed navy blazer and button-down oxford shirt with red and blue regimental-striped tie.

When he did not look up, Jennifer paused for a moment to plan her strategy. Then, she pushed a chair from behind a student desk as close to his as possible and sat down, demurely pulling her skirt down to cover her knees.

"Well now, what can I do for you?" Mr. Herrick said in a disinterested voice, still not looking away from his book.

Jennifer opened a folder and pulled out a book report she had written for his English class the previous week. There was a bright green "C" on the front page with "See me" written beside it. She knew darn well her report wasn't as bad as that, and so did he; Jennifer was a straight "A" student. Leaning forward, she placed the report directly on top of the book he was pretending to read.

In one motion he looked up and turned in his swivel chair, inadvertently bumping his knees against hers.

"Oh, I'm sorry," he stammered self-consciously, rubbing her knee vigorously. Just as suddenly, he jerked his hand away, letting it hover between them as though he didn't know what to do with it.

Jennifer picked up her paper and put it in his hand. Clearly, he was an amateur; this was not going the way she had planned because of his awkwardness.

"It's this paper, Mr. Herrick," she said assuming an expression of sincere concern. "I just don't understand why I got such a low mark?"

Pushing his glasses back on his nose, he stared intently at the paper as though seeing it for the first time, slowly flipping through the pages. If he could keep her here without fear of interruption for at least a half an hour while Hicks and Wade worked on their progress reports, he'd be golden. *Jesus, what if he had misinterpreted her come-on attitude?* But no. She'd been deliberately tormenting him since school began.

Whatever had he been thinking when he had contrived this meeting; giving her the "C", knowing she would question it? It was insane to believe that something would come of this. He had never allowed anything to develop with a student before. Besides, he would be a fool to jeopardize his position.

Obviously impatient, Jennifer stood up and moved behind him. Leaning over his shoulder to look at the report, she pushed her breast against his arm, allowing her hair to brush his cheek. This was intentional. He knew it. His whole body tingled.

He looked up.

Their eyes met and held.

"You seem to have missed the point of the assignment," he said, clearing his throat. "There's—there's no depth to your report. You missed the author's message if this is all you, uh..."

Her lips were just one move away. He would like to kiss her so hard it would crush that confident seductive smile off her face.

When Jennifer moved her hand from the arm of the swivel chair and placed it gently on the back of his neck, he jumped to his feet so fast it was as though she had burned him. She looked up at him, startled at his reaction.

He was trapped between Jennifer and the chair, which banged against his leg, springing back from his sudden movement. He put his hands gingerly on her shoulders to move her aside and Jennifer, thinking he had at last made his first advance, put her arms around his waist, tilted her head upward and closed her eyes.

He was right about her. But should he allow this to happen?

That was his last thought before he kissed her. It was a hungry kiss from a man with a tremendous sexual drive which he rarely had the opportunity, or finesse, to pursue. His hands shook and his heart roared in his ears. He stooped awkwardly with knees bent in order to mold his body to hers, feeling a throb in his groin at the excitement as she responded passionately.

His hand traveled down her back and he discovered that she was not wearing a bra. When he hesitantly reached up under her sweater, she twisted her body so suddenly that, without warning, he found his hand on one small firm breast. The nipple was hard. She rotated her hips against him and fluttered her tongue teasingly against his trembling lips. *Oh God, don't tell me this is happening.* He groaned softly with the pain and the pleasure of it.

They continued to stand there, clinging to each other, mostly because neither was sure of what to do next.

He stroked her hair with his still damp hand, dumbfounded

at what had happened. Pulling away, she began to straighten her sweater and put her hair back in order.

When she looked up, Mr. Herrick dropped into his chair and tried to compose himself. "When can I see you again?" he said, his voice strained and anxious.

"In your Monday class," she answered flippantly, a playful smile started at the corner of her mouth.

"What's so funny?" he asked defensively, his thick eyebrows arched like caterpillars. And then as she stared pointedly at the crouch of his gray flannel pants, he realized why she was laughing. Humiliated, he vowed to forget this degrading scene and never allow it to happen again.

"Well, I don't know about you, but I have work to do," Jennifer said gaily. She picked up her books and deliberately left her report on his desk. "I wish you'd think about that mark, Mr. Herrick. I'm sure that now we've discussed it, you might want to reconsider the grade."

He hated the condescending way she patted his arm.

"See you later," she said and disappeared.

Bitch! Taking off his jacket, he hung it over his arm and slunk into the hall like a beaten dog. He might give her the "A" she deserved, but never would he put himself in this position again. He couldn't believe what had just happened.

CHAPTER THREE

With the letter secretly wrapped inside her towel, Nancy walked into the bathroom.

"Hi, Nancy." It was Sheila peeking out from behind the shower curtain. Transferring a large caramel into one cheek, she said thickly, "why don't you come into my room later? My mother sent some homemade stuff, and we're going to gorge ourselves."

"Thanks, Sheila, maybe I will." Nancy retreated into a toilet stall and locked the door. Putting the seat cover down, she settled herself comfortably in her private sanctuary to read her letter at last. The handwriting was unfamiliar. Holding the letter up to the light, she saw that it was addressed to Miss Heather Brock.

Good Lord, it wasn't even for her. "Boy, the laugh's on me," Nancy exclaimed aloud then clapped her hand over her mouth. She listened for a moment until she was satisfied that Sheila was gone from the shower and that she had not been overheard. What a joke. Who would write to her? Whatever made her think that she would have a letter anyway? She was such a fool.

Nancy wondered who had written Heather. She was so quiet that Nancy knew nothing about her. Perhaps it was from her boyfriend. Nancy thought of Philip. He had disappeared from her life, abandoned her along with their child, her baby.

Did he ever think about her? Or their baby? She felt her eyes start to fill. She still had things to do, her Creative Writing homework that was due tomorrow. She didn't want to cry, and she didn't quite understand how her innocuous peek at the letter had led to this. But Nancy was afraid she was about to start sobbing. She felt her body begin to shake and then convulse with hot tears. A lot of them. A year's worth. She reached for a wad of toilet paper, pressed it to her eyes, and blew her nose. I can't give in to this again, she told herself.

Nancy stared at the letter in her hand, turned it over, and looked for a return address. Half the flap was unstuck and almost involuntarily, she slipped her finger under it. The letter opened with very little effort. Without pause, she pulled the piece of paper from the envelope and began to read:

> *My Dear Heather,*
>
> *It hurts me that my first letter to you since vacation must be in a form of reprimand. But I must say what I have to say, and I want an acknowledgement from you.*
>
> *Eleanor is most offended by your obvious lack of affection or even acceptance of her. She has gone far beyond the call of duty, especially considering the fact that you are not actually her own birth child.*
>
> *Why do you still reject her? She is my wife, and therefore, your mother. I ask (demand, if necessary) that you treat her with proper respect and love. How can we have harmony and unity in our family if you refuse to make an effort? Especially now that the baby is on the way.*
>
> *There will be a penalty for each week that passes without a warm, friendly letter from you to your new mother. As I said, it hurts me to handle this situation in such a forceful manner but you have left me no alternative. She is a sensitive woman, so be certain that your letters are sincere. And be sure to tell her how much you are looking forward to the new addition to our family. Your reaction to the news over vacation was not very sincere. Believe me, I know what is best.*
>
> *I hope you are happy in school and are striving for good reports. It would make your mother and me so proud.*
>
> *Our love to you dear,*
>
> *Father*

Nancy sat there for a long time after finishing the letter, more concerned with its contents than the fact that she had read it. Heather's mother must be dead. Nancy cringed as she thought about the times she had wished the same fate for her own. Her mind raced on. Surely Heather's father was asking the impossible, especially if Heather was still mourning her real mother.

Lord. What should she do with the letter? She realized that if she could not explain to herself why she had read it, there was no way she could explain it to Heather. What in heaven's name would she say?

She could flush it down the toilet, she supposed. No one would have to know. But, if she did that, Heather would be unjustly punished for not writing letters she didn't know she had been told to write.

Nancy suddenly felt frantic to get out of the stall. Stuffing the letter into her bathrobe pocket, she unlocked the door with a temporary sense of relief. Not wanting to be alone with her guilt, she decided to go to Sheila's room where she found her, mouth full, busy telling about her most recent conversation with Miss Wade about the dance.

"Hello everyone." Nancy glanced around the room.

Curled on the end of the bed, Karen appeared to be listening. Audrey leaned against the wall looking as though she were about to go somewhere. Jennifer sat on the desk chair with her bare feet drawn up in front of her, polishing her toenails bright red. Heather seemed to be the only one really paying attention to Sheila. She wore her usual polite, but impenetrable expression.

"Help yourself, Nancy," Sheila said, passing her the cookies. "We're having a real orgy with all this food. Homemade Toll House."

"Better take some," Jennifer told her. "Might help get rid of the taste from those eyeballs in pus sauce we had for supper tonight."

Although the thought of the creamed onions made her want to retch, Nancy took two cookies.

"I didn't think they were so bad," Sheila argued. Nancy remembered that she had eaten most of the bowl, and she had obviously enjoyed them.

"It was the shit-cakes with fish in them that got me," Audrey said unexpectedly from the corner of the room.

Karen held her stomach dramatically. "Oh you guys stop or I'll be sick..."

"I don't care what anyone does to me," Audrey said emphatically, arbitrarily changing the subject, "I'm not going to the dance."

"Don't be a retard," Jennifer said impatiently. "What's one miserable night compared to being on Miss Hicks' shit list for the rest of the year?"

Nancy wondered, not for the first time, why she always made comments like that.

"Jen has a point," Heather sighed.

"I agree with Heather," Nancy said. She was thinking of the stolen letter in her pocket and hoped her supportive comment could lessen her crime, even though she had no intentions of going to the dance.

"Well, I'm going to grin and bear it," Sheila decided. "I met a cute boy downtown yesterday. He could be Marlon Brando's brother. Maybe I'll invite him. It would make it so much easier if you could at least meet your date first."

"You can say that again," Karen wrinkled her freckled nose and squinted her green eyes, something she always did when she was not wearing her glasses. She picked up the box of cookies and handed them around. Sheila looked like she was worried that there might not be any left.

"Of course you could always invite The Creep," Jennifer suggested.

They all laughed.

"Then, at least you'd know what you were getting and no one would bird-dog your date, that's for sure!"

Because of Jennifer, everyone could envision The Creep dancing. Nancy envied her gift with words.

"Yeah," Audrey added with a sneer. "It's like a real cattle

auction. Sign your name and fill out your vital statistics. I bet those birdbrains get a big laugh when their social committee gets our list and they match up dates for us. Sheila has the right idea in inviting a Townie."

Leaning past Sheila, she grabbed a cookie and popped it in her mouth whole.

"You guys forget," said Jennifer. "I would think you'd know by now that Miss Hicks really frowns on us associating with Townies. You better not get caught horsing around with those goons downtown or you'll never get to go shopping again."

"You're right. We debutantes shouldn't even want to associate with the kind of horse manure that can't afford to go to a private school." Audrey said. "As our dear Miss Hicks would put it, 'we have our reputations and honor to protect.'"

Nancy pushed back on Sheila's bed and leaned against the wall. She was in no mood to enter the conversation.

"Well, screw Miss Hicks," Sheila said, nibbling around the edge of another cookie. She looked around the room as though she wanted signs of approval.

"Now, that would be a cold day in hell," Jennifer said, fluttering her eyelashes. Everyone giggled. The idea of Miss Hicks engaged in sex was absurd.

"Since you brought up the subject," Jennifer said dramatically, "I had quite a session with Mr. Herrick tonight."

"I don't believe the skinny jerk has it in him," Audrey said. Nancy agreed although didn't say anything.

"He doesn't...anymore." Jennifer said, laughing.

"I doubt it," Heather said. "he's too refined and intellectual to get involved in a compromising situation."

How like her, Nancy thought, to try to defend the poor man. She would probably defend her father even after he wrote that mean letter.

"Remember ladies," Jennifer said, "a wise woman once said that a stiff prick has no conscience."

"What does that mean?" Karen asked

Nancy stood up. She could not stand one more revolting

remark. "Guess I'll go down to the lounge for a smoke before lights out. Anyone interested?"

No one answered as she opened the door and turned to thank Sheila for the cookies, which were still in her bathrobe pocket.

"Wait a sec, I guess I'll go with you," Heather said as she jumped to her feet.

Lord, of all people it would have to be Heather. On the other hand, it would be the perfect time to tell her about the letter. Just not tonight. No later than Sunday, she told herself firmly.

"Good, let's hurry."

When the two girls passed Miss Wade's apartment, Nancy could see the teacher working diligently at her desk. Thank heavens for small favors, Nancy thought. For tonight, at least, Miss Wade would be too busy to continue her personal crusade for Nancy's religious education.

Miss Wade stacked the papers neatly on her desk and pushed her chair backwards to give herself room enough to stretch her swollen legs. Looking across her sitting room, she strained her eyes to see the clock by her bed in the adjoining room. Ten-thirty, long past lights out...much later than she realized. She decided she'd better make one last corridor check before retiring.

In the annex hallway, Miss Wade stood for a moment to listen before starting her patrol. She knew that the girls often covered the transoms at the top of their doors with a blanket, so she watched the bottom of each girl's door for a possible slice of light. On the way back to her apartment, she paused thoughtfully outside Nancy and Jennifer's room, but heard nothing.

Satisfied that everyone was sleeping, Miss Wade closed her door and locked it securely. She always looked forward to this time of night when she could relax. This was her time to commune with God, and that mattered most of all to her.

She recalled that she had not seen Nancy alone for several days and resolved not to swamp the child by exposing her too rapidly to ideas that could consume her mind and soul. Clearly, the child had not been given a proper spiritual upbringing, she thought with conviction. Imagining what Nancy's home life must have been pained her. She could just picture Nancy's mother...one of those absentee parents who sets a non-moral example for her daughter. No wonder the poor unguided girl got herself with child.

At that thought, a flash of pain crossed the teacher's face and her breathing became difficult. The poor girl must be so thankful to know that God had forgiven her for sinning. She had told Nancy that if she sought God, she would find Him. Without warning, Miss Wade felt her pulse quicken. Warmth spread across her breasts and flowed into her soft, dark nipples. She could feel that familiar sensation at the base of her stomach. It rocked through her groin in rhythmic spasms. "Oh God," she whispered with silent passion, "I am Yours. I live only for You!"

Her energy spent, she staggered and put one hand to her clammy forehead and one on the back of a chair to steady herself. She was sure the doctor was wrong and that these episodes were certainly hot flashes. And yet the sensation was so—so odd. It hurt, yet it was a pleasurable pain. Her heart pounded. She was breathing heavily and her head throbbed. She felt wet all over, even down there. She felt ashamed, but during the entire experience, she had known that she was with God.

I know Him, she thought. I have felt His touch.

The dizziness passed. Her hair clung to her forehead in moist tight curls. She was thankful that these perplexing episodes only seemed to happen in the privacy of her own sitting room.

Thank you God, for that.

She would be most embarrassed if her students or colleagues suspected that she was entering menopause at this point in her life. She didn't care that the doctor explained something about overly sensitive genitalia, or some such nonsense. She knew what it is. The change of life. Plain and simple.

Miss Wade took off her clothes, deliberately avoiding the mirror, and dropped the damp garments into the hamper. Adjusting the water, she stepped into the shower. She had to be careful when she lifted her mammoth legs to avoid slipping. Every evening without fail, after communing with God and feeling His touch, Miss Wade took a shower. She was a most fastidious person, and after cleansing her soul, she cleansed her body.

After a bitterly cold January, February was warmer with only a few patches of snow remaining in shaded areas of the school grounds.

Four days had passed and Nancy still had Heather's letter.

She watched from the window of her room as groups of girls headed off in different directions on their usual Sunday afternoon walks. She knew she must be the only one who always walked alone. Even Sheila and Audrey went together in spite of their differences. She saw Mr. and Mrs. Packer wheeling their baby in a carriage. It was a little girl, and she realized with a pang that their baby was about the same age as hers would have been. Was. Is.

You'll learn to follow rules you may not necessarily like. You can't begin too quickly, the director of the Florence Crittendon House had said to Nancy after her mother left her there. Thus began the regime of eating, exercising, counseling, and studying for exams sent by her teachers. No instruction on how to change a diaper or nurse a baby. Just sign the papers and go home. Empty and despairing.

You'll be home in plenty of time to do your Christmas shopping, and appreciate the joy of the season with your family.

As Nancy watched the Packers pass beneath her window, she wondered if they'd let her sit for them. She decided to offer the next time she was assigned to the Packer's dining table.

Maybe she and Heather could even baby-sit together. That was, if Heather could forgive her for having opened the letter.

Turning back to her room, Nancy reached under her mattress for Heather's letter, and then resolutely stepped into the hall. She tapped softly on Heather's door, but her silent prayer was that there would be no answer.

"Come in."

Just her luck. Although her determination faltered, she proceeded to do what she knew she must. She opened the door and smiled hesitantly at Heather who was stretched out across her bed, an open book lying on her chest and a stuffed kitten sitting on top of it. The kitten looked as though it had been loved for many years. Maybe it was one her mother had given her.

"If you're busy, I'll come back later," Nancy said, wanting to run in the other direction.

"Oh no, please come in." Heather jumped to her feet. She dumped books and clothes off a chair so Nancy had a place to sit. "Actually, I was hoping for a break from the books."

The two girls sat in silence for a moment, each searching for something interesting to say.

"How do you like the school now that you've been here a while?" Heather asked.

I can't take this, Nancy thought. She was desperate to escape without answering Heather's question, without getting involved. However, she took a deep ragged breath, reached in her pocket for the letter, and thrust it toward its rightful owner.

"What's this?"

"It's yours. It was in my box. I opened it by mistake."

"It's from my father!" Heather exclaimed, turning the letter over to open it. She hesitated only for a moment when she saw the unsealed flap.

Nancy knew the contents by heart. Embarrassed, she avoided looking directly at Heather. She knew her smile would not last long. Nancy hated all parents in general. Now she was a "Peeping Tom".

Heather stood and stumbled toward the window. Nancy looked at her stocky figure silhouetted against the afternoon sun slanting through the window, illuminating her golden curls like a halo. Her shoulders shook slightly and Nancy realized that she was weeping silently.

Nancy wanted to be anywhere but right there in Heather's room. "I was just going out for a walk," she said, "would you like to come along?" Even though Heather murmured that she would, Nancy knew that she had to complete her confession before they left.

"Heather, I...I have to tell you that I read the letter. It's hard to explain why because I really didn't mean to do it. I realize that you don't know me well enough to believe it, but I swear to you no one will ever hear about what he said from me. I just wanted you to know."

When Heather did not answer, Nancy went to her room and armed herself with coat and scarf. She was not sure that Heather would go with her, but there she was, already waiting outside her door. Her expression was indefinable. No tears, no smile, just blank.

The two girls walked for more than an hour in complete silence. When they came to a fork in the road, there was no conference as to which way to go yet neither girl missed a step as they each chose the same direction. Their gait was brisk as though moving toward a definite destination together. They made no stops until they arrived back at the school using the rear entrance because it was closer to their rooms.

Nancy watched Heather climb a few steps ahead of her. What would happen next? As if answering, Heather opened her bedroom door and stepped in without a backward glance. She closed the door behind her.

Well, it was over. Nancy was sure that Heather hated her. She slept miserably that night imagining that she could hear her crying.

Nancy was wrong. Heather did not cry, but she did not sleep either. Much later, somewhere between sleep and wakefulness, Heather asked herself, why? repeatedly. What had she done to lose her father's love?

Heather remembered the day just after her fourteenth birthday, when the family doctor told her that her mother had muscular dystrophy. He had explained that she was rapidly losing control of her muscles and would soon be confined to her bed.

"Yes, she's going to die," he said, "but Heather, self-pity and tears are not appropriate. There'll be plenty of time for that when your mother is gone. Right now, you must act cheerful around her. There will be a fulltime nurse from here on to help you and your father. Actually, it's your father I'm really concerned about. You've got to keep your feelings to yourself and think of him."

As she tried to choke back her sobs, Heather had prayed; "Oh, please God, make Daddy want me." Heather never cried in front of anyone after the doctor delivered his prognosis. Her emotions were too raw for that. It was too dangerous to think about it. From that day forward, she centered her life around her father. Mrs. Brock and her nurse seemed to exist in a world apart from them.

Dejected, her father had allowed self-pity to overwhelm him and because she wanted so badly to help him, Heather had become a chameleon. She was someone who was willing to become what ever he wanted her to be. And in the process, as she knew now, she had lost track of who she really was.

Only at night when she experienced brutal terrifying nightmares did the shy retiring child she had been before her mother's illness return.

The first time Harold Brock had heard his daughter's agonized cries, he had stumbled out of his bed and hurried to her room where he soon found the only way to comfort her was by lying down beside her. Running his hand through her golden curls, he would gently stroke her forehead until gradually

Heather's cries would become whimpers. Then she would fall into a peaceful sleep. This ritual became a necessary crutch for both father and daughter. Heather grew to depend on the warmth of her father's body curled against hers to give her the equanimity that she needed to get through each day.

For Harold Brock, those peaceful interludes gave him a strange yet welcome feeling of power and strength. It pleased him to know he had the ability to pacify his daughter. It fed his parched ego. It made him feel manly, and it had been a long time since he had felt that. For eight months, they had never been happier.

The bliss lasted until Mrs. Brock died. Harold Brock's "legal" freedom made him restless. He spent more time away from home...and Heather. He began to escort eligible women, soon concentrating his attention on a widow named Eleanor Yeager.

Shaken by these memories, Heather threw back her covers. Pulling her down puff off the bed, she wrapped it around her shoulders and knelt before the window. Outside, on the dark side of dawn, she saw the first snowflakes of the storm. Perhaps it was an omen...for what, she wasn't sure.

Heather cringed at the memory of the devastating day when her entire world abruptly ended in stark reality. This was the day her father had introduced her to his soon-to-be fiancée.

"I'm so happy to meet you, Mrs. Yeager," she had said. But that night, Heather had screamed at her bewildered father, "I thought you loved me."

He stood by her bed where he had so often offered and received comfort. "I assumed you'd be as pleased as I am at the thought of having a woman around the house again," he had said. When she finally cried, it seemed that she would never stop. Her father had wiped his sweaty hands on his pants and tried to soothe her, tenderly stroking her arm, but she had darted away, striking out at him angrily.

"Don't touch me, you liar," she cried. "I thought you loved me. Well, I despise you. I hate you. Do you hear? Hate. Hate!"

Badly frightened, Harold Brock had quickly backed out of

the room and ran, half stumbling, to telephone the doctor who immediately suggested boarding school "where Heather could form normal associations with girls of her own age and interests as well as get a good education in her senior year."

Not trusting himself to make the final decision, Harold Brock had followed the doctor's suggestion. Mrs. Yeager had agreed that it was the only way to handle the situation. After all, they had reasoned, it was unnatural for Heather to be that possessive, although her father was sheepishly flattered.

Now Heather could not think about this too long, the memories were too painful. She tried to concentrate on the scene before her. She kneeled up to the window and gazed at the snow that had snapped down over the frozen field like a bed sheet. It was a clean, orderly world.

CHAPTER FOUR

The girls squealed with delight when they discovered that it had been snowing throughout the night. When Nancy returned to her room from the bathroom, a stray snowball hit her squarely between her shoulders. Startled, she screamed. Nightgowns flying, the girls scattered to hide in their rooms.

Recognizing the swishing sound of Miss Wade's approach, Nancy tried to escape into her room, but someone was holding the door. She was trapped until Heather opened hers, and pulled Nancy inside.

"Hiding makes no difference to me," they heard Miss Wade say, "I know what's going on, and I want it to stop. Do you girls hear? You better be getting dressed for breakfast. Mondays go on as usual, snow or no snow." Nancy hunched behind the door with Heather. There were no answers and definitely no snickering until they heard Miss Wade's door slam shut.

"The coast is clear," Heather cried. "Hurry up and get dressed so we can go down to find out whose table we've been assigned to for the week." With relief, Nancy realized that Heather had forgiven her for reading the letter. And maybe even more, maybe she wanted a special friend, too. It would change everything for Nancy. She could feel something inside her letting go. The pain and isolation that had been her life for the past year began to ease and it was with a lighter step, she rushed to her room to get dressed.

Wednesday already, and the coward had not made one

single move, Jennifer thought as she picked up her comb and made angry swipes at her hair. She supposed he thought he had made a bad mistake and wanted to call it off now. Well she wouldn't let that happen. No wonder the girls didn't believe her. He had not even looked at Jennifer since that Friday. But now she knew for certain that he had no chance against her wiles. He'd be back for more, a lot more.

Going in search of her sneakers, Jennifer saw that Nancy had placed them neatly in the closet. Christ, you wouldn't even know she had a roommate considering how little she saw of her. Ha! That was a pun. She thought her little roomy would flip if any of the girls ever saw her undressed. *What made her act like such a prude, anyway?* She pretended that everything was terribly shocking to her, but Jennifer bet that the sweet, demure, big-brown-eyed doll was just as ready for some action as the rest of the girls. She wondered what she and Heather found to talk about all the time. It escaped her why anyone would want to spend so much time with Heather anyway. Jennifer stood on her toes to see more of herself in the small mirror. On impulse, she removed her gym blouse and stood naked to the waist in the middle of her bedroom. Taking a red sleeveless sweater from her drawer, she pulled it down carefully over her hair, hesitating a moment to wonder if it might be too tight. But no, she told herself. She wanted him to see them bounce during gym class. Looking at her watch, she dashed from the room on her way to the gymnasium.

Turning a corner in the passageway, Jennifer bumped squarely into Mr. Jones, who was wiping down the walls.

"Oh, I'm sorry Mr. Jones. Are you all right?" She received no answer. It was as though she weren't there. The creep, she thought, and rushed off, hating the fact that she had actually brushed against him. Ugh!

Mr. Jones was convinced that Jennifer, well, actually most of the girls, secretly liked him even if they did call him The Creep behind his back. He didn't care. The idea was an aphrodisiac. All he had to do was keep the place clean. He loved this house. To him it was not a school, it was a mansion filled with guests. And he was its caretaker.

For the most part, he was rarely lonely. The guests never knew that it was he who placed wild flowers in their rooms whenever he could and there was no need for them to know. He knew, and that was enough. They also didn't know that it was he who took a pair of panties now and then as a reward for his kindnesses. *Maybe some knew and even liked it.* After all, although they might not know it, they owed him a great deal. And so far, he had claimed very little in return.

Jonathan Herrick walked out of the equipment room and kicked the door shut behind him. Dropping an armful of volleyballs, he watched them scatter across the floor. Five minutes more before the stampede, he thought, as he picked up the schedule. Pushing his glasses on his nose, he glanced down the list to Wednesday. Jennifer's name leaped out at him.

Jonathan had never dreamed that he would want anyone so much that he ached. But Jennifer haunted him day and night. It was appalling. The worst part of it was that she knew he wanted her. He had seen the way she watched him over the top of a book in study hall and how she started arriving early in his English class so she could get a front seat. Maybe he would have a talk with her after class, reason with her, and let her know that they were in an impossible situation. He'd be strong.

It was agonizing to know she was there, available for the taking. Kicking one of the balls viciously across the room, he watched it spin into the corner and drift lazily back toward him. Every time he was tempted to make an advance, he remembered how much he needed this teaching position. It represented years of working nights to put himself through college and graduate school. Years of dedication to this one goal. Jesus, it would be so stupid for him to jeopardize his job just for a few moments of satisfaction.

The bell interrupted his thoughts as a swarm of identically dressed girls, all in light and dark blue uniforms, bounded into the gym across Mr. Jones's highly polished floor. He reminded himself that he had to send anyone who ignored the rule that required sneakers in the gym to Miss Hicks since Mr. Jones acted as though the teachers were personally responsible for any marks the girls made on the gym floor. Not that he ever said anything. That obsequious little oddball just mumbled to himself.

He felt for the whistle that hung from his neck. He put it between his dry lips and then blew loudly for attention. The high-pitched din reduced itself quickly to a respectful undertone. "Choose teams for volleyball," he shouted. "Brock and Vaughan are acting captains."

They were calling out names when Jennifer came dashing through the door, hair flying. He busied himself adjusting the scoreboard until the teams cheered and split into two groups. Finally, he looked up and saw a mass of different colored heads, blue torsos, and white legs with one red sweater in their midst that was so tight it boggled his mind.

Mr. Herrick's eyes blinked unbelievingly behind his thick glasses when his sweeping glance rested on Jennifer.

Oh Jesus, why did she do it? She knew the strict rules about wearing uniforms to the gym. She knew he'd be forced to question her in front of the entire class. Shit! Taking a deep breath, he wiped a line of sweat from his upper lip.

"Miss Stewart," he said curtly. "May I ask why you are not wearing your complete uniform?"

"I couldn't find it," Jennifer replied. "Honestly."

"That's not much of an excuse now, is it, Miss Stewart?" He found that he was secretly enjoying the public rebuke; payback for catching him so completely off guard two weeks ago in his classroom. It had been so humiliating.

She smiled ruefully, "I'm sorry, Mr. Herrick."

"Sorry isn't good enough," he replied. "See me after this period."

"Yes sir." Turning her back to the others, she winked at him.

"Now, let's get this game started," he said. She was unstoppable. He had to put an end to it. Why did she do things like that, he asked himself, not for the first time. He was not accustomed to girls having crushes on him like some other teachers might have been and he certainly was not prepared for this outrageous flirtation. *Was she making fun of him?*

Jennifer played a vigorous game, deliberately flaunting herself in front of him until all he could see were her bouncing breasts.

Jonathan Herrick's eyes fixated on the large clock over the door. Would this period end, he asked himself. *Look at her. Just look at her perform. Why in heaven's name had he told her to stay after class?* When the bell finally rang, he thanked God for small mercies.

The girls rushed from the gym. Their loud chatter receded as they headed to their rooms to shower, change, and get ready for the afternoon study period.

How should he handle this? Stalling, Jonathan Herrick sauntered around the gym picking up balls, all too aware that Jennifer was still there. Suddenly, the volleyball she had been holding, hit him squarely between the shoulders. He stumbled forward into the equipment room and dropped the balls in their bin. Without warning, the door banged shut. He spun around, glad for an excuse to feel anger rather than desire.

"Did you want to see me, Mr. Herrick?" Jennifer asked.

Jesus! How could she play the innocent like this? He was frantic. They stared at each other.

"Yes, I did. But first of all, what was the idea of hitting me with that ball?"

"I'm sorry. It was a mistake. Did you, or didn't you want to see me?"

"Yes. It's about that sweater, you know..." His voice broke off, uncertain of what to say next.

"You mean this one?" she asked, while with one swift movement, she grasped her sweater at the waistline, pulled it up over her head, and threw it at him. Without thinking, he caught it.

"Jennifer, why do you do these things?" he moaned, unable to take his eyes off her nakedness.

"Because I want you to want me." Jennifer approached him slowly.

"I want you," he said, trying to keep his voice from quivering. "You know I want you more than anything in the world, but it's not right."

"Show me you want me and then I'll believe you," Jennifer said as she unbuttoned his shirt.

"Jennifer, we mustn't," he pleaded helplessly, as she pulled open his shirt and slid her arms around him. Feeling her breasts against his bare skin, he succumbed, and tossed her sweater to the floor.

"Wait a minute," she said breathlessly. "Pull one of those mats down." He grabbed one from the top of the pile. "Yes, that's right."

Simultaneously they sank to their knees, facing one another. Jennifer took his hands and placed them on her breasts.

"So soft..." he moaned.

Jonathan thought he might faint when she worked at the buckle of his pants, and then tugged them downward. Collapsed on the mat, he lay watching her, his whole body throbbing.

She discarded the rest of her clothes and she kissed him, sliding her tongue into his mouth. As the kiss intensified, they pressed closer against each other until, unable to wait any longer, he entered her, groaning as her body closed around him. They climaxed together just as he drew away from her. She fell back, shaking and weak. Eyes closed, he breathed heavily.

"You didn't need to do that." Jennifer's voice was far away. "I can't get pregnant. Please don't ask me why now. I'll tell you about it later."

As they clasped each other again, arms and legs entangled,

a sudden draft swept under the door. Jennifer shivered and pressed herself closer to him.

"I'm starting to feel nervous," he told her, "we'd better get our clothes on." They dressed quickly, Jonathan openly watching Jennifer.

Seeing her red sweater on the floor brought him back to reality. "What are we going to do?" he asked.

"We're going to do this every chance we get," she told him. "That was great. I never thought sex would be like that!"

"Well, maybe occasionally and with discretion."

"Occasionally? Did you enjoy it or not? Even if you said no, I wouldn't believe you. Besides, you couldn't perform like that without loving every minute of it. The only way to keep me happy is to keep me satisfied. Think you can do that?"

She must have read that line somewhere recently, he thought. Wasn't it from *God's Little Acre*? He'd seen it being passed around during study hall with brown paper over the cover. Or maybe it was just out of *True Confessions*. He guessed that was a more likely source.

"So, it's just a matter of where and when," Jennifer told him, pulling on her sweater. "I know we can arrange that to the full satisfaction of both parties. But first things first, I'm going to be late to study hall if I don't hurry. Oh, and by the way Mr. Herrick, please forget to give me a demerit for my not turning up with a complete gym uniform. I've got two this month already."

Knowing he was a fool, guessing that she might be using him, he put his hand lightly on her shoulder, wanting to prolong her departure. "Where can we meet next? And when?"

He hated it when she was so off handed. He wanted, God how he wanted to continue, but at what cost?

"How about Sunday at your place?" She suggested boldly.

"Would we dare? Could you make it without being seen?" His spirits rose at the prospect of having her all to himself in the security of his bachelor's cottage on the edge of the school grounds.

"Leave that to me. You just be there."

"What time?"

"How should I know? Whenever I can make it. Don't forget to put the mat away," she said with a wicked wink.

As he bent to pick it up, she bolted from the room, banging the door open as she left.

Why did she always leave doors open after her, he wondered, suddenly annoyed. It made him feel so damned exposed. But everything would be better at the cottage, he assured himself. Perhaps she would be less likely to mock him there.

However, it made him feel uneasy that she was so flippant. What would he do if Miss Hicks ever found out about them? He shook his head.

Did she care about him?

Jonathan Herrick resigned himself that they were indeed having a secret affair. He knew he could not lose his head again, but he also knew he would. The anticipation was heady. Jesus, she was barely eighteen years old but she made him feel as though he never lived before. She was unbelievable and he was putting everything, his life as he knew it, on the line for her. He needed to be cautious and in control, but how?

Nancy was thrilled to have found a close friend at Winthrop Academy at last and she knew now that Heather felt the same way. First they had begun to wait for one another after a class. Then they had started to sit together in study hall. Now they were on the same team in basketball.

However, Nancy's baby would always be her secret no matter how close she became to Heather. And she also knew that Heather would not tell about the resentment she felt toward her father and stepmother for sending her away from home. Both of them would jealously guard their secrets.

One day after gym, the two girls lounged lazily in Heather's room, too exhausted to change out of their gym suits.

"Phew, what a session that was," Nancy said, holding out

the front of her gym blouse, flapping it back and forth to cool herself.

"Basketball gets so darn frantic," Heather replied. "Instead of playing, I feel like I'm just getting out of everyone's way."

The girls enjoyed a comfortable silence.

Nancy was surprised when Heather suddenly burst out with: "I owe it to my father at least, to explain that letter to you."

"Well, go ahead if you want to," Nancy said, thinking of her mother and how hard it would be to explain *her* to someone. "But believe me; it's probably impossible to explain anything parents do."

"People are not always the way they seem," Heather told her. "Take your roommate for example."

"You take her," Nancy replied, "I've had about enough."

"Jennifer thinks it's a big deal to talk cheap," Heather continued, "but, you know what? I bet she's never even been to bed with a boy."

Heather said this with such conviction that Nancy had to reconsider.

"Okay," Nancy said, "you could be right. But how can she say the things she does with such authority? And everyone's afraid of her sharp tongue. She doesn't mind putting anyone down just to get a good laugh."

And if she ever finds out about me, she would probably crucify me.

"That's exactly what I mean," Heather said triumphantly. "Maybe underneath, she's not like that at all. I mean, even if she'd like to relax and act natural, she can't anymore."

"Like she's caught between what she'd like to be and the way people expect her to be?" Nancy was almost convinced.

"Yes. Yes, that's it." Heather was excited that Nancy got her point. "Now, if you can see that, I think you'll be able to understand how my father got himself into just such a predicament. He married Mrs. Yeager thinking it would please me. But it didn't."

"When did your mother die, Heather?"

"Almost two years ago. Actually, it's weird. I mean, it was the night before President Eisenhower sent troops to Little Rock to protect those Negro kids. That seemed more important than my own mother's death because she had been sick for so long." Nancy wanted to wrap her arms around her friend. "Oh Nancy, I loved my father so completely and then all of a sudden my mom died and he didn't care anymore"...Heather's voice broke as she struggled to keep from crying.

"I think you're wrong about this." Nancy said emphatically. "Wouldn't a man with a child want a mother for her and a wife for himself?"

Nancy groaned inwardly, thinking she sounded like her mother's friends when they came over for bridge. 'Playing psychologists,' she had always called it.

"You're just quoting what adults would say," Heather declared vehemently. "My dad hardly left the house. His only thoughts were of me. And I'm not being self-centered 'cause it was mutual."

"I'm sure he loves you just as much as always," Nancy told her. "He probably got married thinking it would please you, and now you're forcing him to choose between you and his wife." It occurred to Nancy that it was ironic that she should sound so mature when she was counseling Heather. Like Joannie. Too bad she couldn't counsel herself as well.

Heather was silent for a long time. "Maybe you're right," she finally conceded. "But everything was great without her."

"Well, if you want your father to be happy, maybe you could try to warm up to her."

Heather shrugged. "I guess so."

Nancy shuffled through clutter on Heather's desk for a pen. "Come on," she said, "let's write a *really* sincere, *really* friendly letter back to her."

"Don't you think it's too late? I'm not even sure what to call her." Heather sat back on her chair, dejected. "Oh hell, I can't do it."

"How about Mother Brock?" Nancy asked mischievously.

"That sounds like a mother-in-law. No, I guess I'd call her by her first name. Eleanor."

Nancy passed her a clipboard, complete with a sheet of blank paper. She leaned forward, her hair almost hiding her face from view, as she watched while Heather wrote; *Dear Eleanor...*

"Now what?" Her anticipation was a palpable energy. "I am so glad my letter got into your box, Nancy. It makes everything bearable to be able to share with someone."

Taking her father's letter, Heather tore it into small pieces and threw it in the air. The scraps scattered like snowflakes settling to the floor.

"Me too," Nancy told her wistfully. "Come on now. Let's make this letter a good one. Old Eleanor will like you in spite of herself after getting all these sincere letters we're going to write."

❧

Miss Hicks stood in her favorite spot by the front window of her office and stared down at the banks of snow piled high on either side of the driveway. She had never seen February bring so much winter before. She bent to smooth her stockings over her spindly legs, and then checked the alignment of the seams in the mirror.

Winter made her feel old. It always had done that to her, even when she was a young girl. It made no sense, but so many events in life were senseless. She shrugged, and then examined her face closely. So far this year, there were no new lines. She was fortunate to have carried the school through to February without any major problems.

Now, if they could just get past this tiresome Spring Dance without a catastrophe, they would be doing well. She dreaded these social functions. If she had her way, they'd be eliminated. But, oh no, the girls wanted even more of them. It was like the smoking privileges they finally wrangled out of her. They had managed to survive the Christmas dance, but the one coming up was even worse.

From habit, Miss Hicks massaged her temples. She did not know what happened to the girls in the springtime, but it never failed. They got such foolish ideas into their heads. Spring was bad enough, but to have a dance too. It was always a potential disaster.

The headmistress shivered. Two years ago, Miss Wade had discovered that a student and her date had slipped away from the spring dance and disappeared into the cool evening. It had been a bad year. They expelled that foolish girl. Then there was the girl that Miss Wade had caught smoking in the woods. Even though that poor woman was truly reluctant to turn in a student, she followed school policy scrupulously. That was what made her a good employee. She and Sam were fond of Miss Wade.

And there was Paul. She was glad to be able to give him a safe place to live and work. He always stayed low, did his job, and kept out of the way. She wondered if he would report a student who broke school rules. He had, she knew, a soft heart beneath that misshapen exterior. She was aware that the girls called him "The Creep." God forbid that they ever learned more about him.

Well, so far, there was nothing to speak of this year. Heartened, Miss Hicks knocked on the door of the adjoining room. "Sam," she called, "it's time for dinner."

"Hold on a minute, I'll be right with you." Sam's voice was edged with irritation, probably at being rushed.

"My dear, you work so hard. Now stop and come along, I'm anxious to get dinner started so we can launch into the meeting directly afterwards."

The two women descended the stairs to the dining room, shoulders bumping as they walked out of rhythm.

After dinner, the entire student body filed quietly into the reception hall. Miss Hicks knew they whispered and speculated about the subject matter of the meeting. She had great influence over those in her charge, and the idea made her powerful.

A hush followed Miss Hicks as she walked to the front of the room. "Please do sit down girls."

She waited for them to settle on the thick oriental carpet.

Mr. Jones had roped off most of the chairs in the room because they were antiques too precious for students to use. He was almost as fastidious with the academy as she was, and seemed to understand her concern that: "Girls have difficulty learning to act like ladies," something he must have heard her say many times.

"Good evening ladies," Miss Hicks said, smiling thinly.

"Good evening, Miss Hicks," the girls replied in unison.

"I shan't keep you long, but there are a few matters I wish to discuss. It has come to my attention that food continues to disappear from the kitchen despite repeated warnings. Now it seems to me that since there is plenty of food served at meals, there is no excuse for this disgraceful situation. I consider this a violation of trust that the faculty places in the students and the perpetrator will be punished accordingly if there should be another occurrence."

Miss Hicks cast a severe look at the innocent, upturned faces. "To continue on the minus side, I would like to remind you that we do not allow snowball fights in the buildings."

An outburst of snickering swept across the room.

"This may seem amusing to you," Miss Hicks said, frowning, "but it creates extra work for those who must mop up after you and replace broken window panes. Mr. Jones, I'm sure, must have some limitation to his infinite patience concerning your pranks and their aftermath. Let's show him more consideration, shall we?" Miss Hicks looked up at the ceiling as though her list of grievances appeared there.

"The laundry reports that there have been lipstick stains on the napkins during the week. This disturbs me greatly since students are permitted to wear make-up only on Sundays and special occasions. I shan't go on about the background of this rule but please remember that it is best to be natural at all times so that your friends know you, and not a facade." Pausing for this thought to penetrate, Miss Hicks scanned the back of the room until she located Sam. Dear, loyal Sam. Whatever would she do without Sam? Their eyes locked for a moment. Miss

Hicks took note of which faculty members had taken the time to attend the meeting. She was pleased at the turnout.

"We are halfway through the school year and yet *some* girls still continue to whisper during Vespers. You know who you are and that this is forbidden. I'll say no more. Now then, although mid-semester exams are not facing us for another month, it is none too soon to begin preparing for them. You mustn't forget that they are not only a test of memory and knowledge, but hard work, long hours of study, fortitude, integrity, and above all, honesty. We must fortress ourselves now for the trials ahead."

"And seniors. I know you visited colleges over Christmas vacation. I wish to remind you to see your counselors for help in filling out the applications. Don't procrastinate, Ladies. This is your future."

Miss Hicks cleared her throat, as she attempted to clarify her thoughts on the next subject.

"On the plus side of my agenda, I would like to commend the students who *do* have a superb record of promptness over the last three weeks. It is evident that a sincere effort has been made to always be on time, a true virtue. Therefore it pleases me to announce that no one will have to forfeit her downtown privileges for the coming week."

Looking down at her watch, Miss Hicks noted that she had ten more minutes in which to talk about the dance and answer any questions.

"Lastly, I would like to bring up the subject of the dance with The Bryant School. I understand that their social committee has requested that our list be completed and sent to them by the weekend. You are not required to attend, although you all know how I feel about it, so you may act according to your consciences. The boys have once again asked that you not put down fictitious information concerning yourself on the sign-up sheet. When their committee attempts to match you up with a boy of similar height and interests, it becomes impossible to do so successfully if we do not supply them with the truth. The lists will be removed from the board Friday night. Are there any questions?"

There was absolute silence. Miss Hicks knew that the girls avoided eye contact, not wanting to be called upon to speak.

"Now we'll adjourn this meeting so you have time to contemplate the important points we have discussed tonight."

The girls clapped, not from appreciation but rather from habit and relief that the meeting was over.

Miss Hicks with head bent, walked purposefully around the group of girls struggling to their feet and escaped up the stairs to her apartment. She was pleased that the talk had gone so well and she smiled to herself when she overheard Jennifer say, "Miss Hicks should write a book called, *Words to Live By: Two Hundred Pages of Solid Quotes."*

They were her girls, she thought affectionately. All of them. And when they left Winthrop, they would all be the kind of young ladies that even her grandmother would have been proud of.

CHAPTER FIVE

That same night the girls congregated in their lounge, smoked fiendishly, and complained about the dance.

"Oh my, we have such marvelous school spirit, Hilda, my dear," Sheila said, mimicking Miss Hicks. "Do you realize we have one hundred percent turnout for our dance? The girls just love the Academy so much that they wouldn't dream of missing a school function. And they're going voluntarily, too. Just imagine we didn't have to break one neck or twist one arm."

The enthusiastic reception of her comment delighted Sheila. She reached in her bathrobe pocket for another Tootsie Roll. Jennifer, deep in the only comfortable chair, merely grunted.

Audrey twisted around in her chair and dangled her legs awkwardly over the arm. "If the consequences weren't so dreadful, I wouldn't go near one of those dances with a ten foot pole," she said. "A real horror show, that's what I call them. Can't you see it now? I'll be paired up with some jerk that'll come up to my belly button." She pushed her short straight hair behind her ear as she mimicked Miss Hicks' well known gesture. "Of course the boys never lie on *their* sign up sheets."

"Let us not forget our own dear Mr. Jones and all his patience with us naughty girls," Jennifer said as she clicked her Zippo shut and blew a mouthful of smoke at the ceiling. "He is so sensitive that we must at all cost preserve his delicate feelings. Perhaps if we are extra 'specially good to him, he might reward us by taking a bath semi-annually instead of annually. Or at least get some deodorant. Why, he might even say a few words of gratitude."

Everyone in the room made a face or some guttural utterance of agreement.

"Yes, he sure does stink."

"That's the understatement of the century."

"Hicks doesn't know her ass from her elbow," Audrey announced. "If she knew half of what goes on around here, her I.Q. might break eighty. She gives us all that happy horse-shit and doesn't even know the score herself."

Jennifer had just been thinking about her encounter with Mr. Herrick, how safe she felt when he had wrapped his arms around her. Now she decided *not* to tell the girls. She sensed that this relationship might be different. It could lead into something really special for both of them. She knew it would be a stupid betrayal to blab about it to her friends.

"You may be wrong," Sheila said in a conspiratorial manner. "They say that Hicks had a very unhappy love affair when she was young. As a matter of fact, I heard that she got pregnant and the guy refused to marry her so she gave the baby away. Maybe that's why Miss Hicks hired Mr. Packer when it was obvious that his wife was going to have a baby."

"Sheila, how can you spread such a vicious rumor?" Nancy's eyes flashed angrily. "How in heaven's name can you know anything as personal as that about Miss Hicks? And if you don't know it, then you have a colossal nerve to be saying something like that on...on speculation. Or did you say it to merely sound amusing?" Nancy's hands shook when she lit a Kool.

"I can't imagine that about Miss Hicks either." Heather looked at Nancy with concern. Something had upset her. That was obvious. But what?

"Jeez, I was only repeating what I heard," Sheila said, wide eyed. She never expected comments from the usually soft-spoken Nancy, or Heather for that matter.

"Well, where do you get all your information anyway?" Heather asked, trying to give Nancy time to regain her composure.

"I'm very friendly with Sam, and as you know," Sheila said, "she's a direct pipeline."

"Maybe you're too friendly with Sam," Audrey suggested. "Miss Hicks wouldn't like that."

Jennifer was the only one who laughed.

"Miss Sampson never opened her mouth to you or anyone, especially about Miss Hicks," Heather continued earnestly. "You're fabricating the whole story. Everyone knows you do it all the time."

"Oh, for Christ sakes, what did I say to deserve this?" Sheila looked around the room for support.

Audrey glared at her. "Sheila, you stupid shit," she mumbled, pulling on her middle finger until it cracked. "You really put your foot in it this time. Leave her alone, you guys," she said aloud. "You all know she just likes to hear herself talk."

Nancy jammed her cigarette into the ashtray. "I don't have to listen to such trash." She said, starting toward the door.

"Why the big panic? What's everyone having such a big hemorrhage over? All I said was...."

"For god-almighty-sakes will you shut up, Sheila?" Audrey warned.

The door slammed behind Nancy.

"Each and every one of you is a horse's ass," Jennifer said in a disgusted voice.

"You know, it just occurred to me why she got so fired up." Sheila appeared amazed at her own intuition.

"The light dawns even over the head of the biggest retard in the school." Jennifer blew a perfect smoke ring. "Christ, Sheila, you must need a church to fall on you, you idiot." After her reaction to the story about Miss Hicks, Jennifer thought the rumors about Nancy having had a baby might be true. Now, maybe she could get her little roomy to talk about it.

"That's another one of your lies," said Heather in defense of Nancy.

"Will you all just shut up? SHUT UP!" Audrey threw her cigarette on the floor grinding it out with her sneaker, very much aware that it was against the rules of the lounge. She didn't care. The Creep could clean it up.

Smoke from their cigarettes gathered in the far corner of

the room. The glow from the lamp gave it a distant lavender hue as it coiled and spun in the light.

Nancy was locked in the bathroom stall when she heard Heather call her name. She had been so grateful to Heather when she came to her defense in the lounge. Nancy pitied Miss Hicks. Those girls didn't care how their words hurt people or how intrusive their curiosity could be. She had been blessed with Heather's friendship; she was the sister that Joannie never had been.

"Nancy, my dear," Miss Wade called from the head of the corridor. "If you're free, perhaps we can have a little talk."

Nancy sighed and rubbed her forehead. Lord, why couldn't she have made it back to her room from the bathroom before being seen? She just could not bear another session with her tonight.

"Well actually, Miss Wade," she said, "I was on my way to bed. I have a headache."

"Fine. Fine. You get ready for bed and we'll meet in my sitting room in ten minutes." The teacher turned away, not waiting for an answer.

Shit, shit, shit! Nancy kicked open her door and threw herself on her bed, tears rolling down her pale cheeks and into her hair. What should she do? If those gossip mongers ever found out about her baby, she'd be the brunt of every joke in the school. Miss Wade knew. Yet it was supposed to be confidential. If Waddles would just leave her alone! She sat up, rubbing her eyes. Good ole Waddles should sit in on one of their bitching sessions in the lounge. It would shock about five pounds off each leg. Nancy smiled in spite of herself. Well, I can't keep our 'Mother Superior' waiting. Dragging her feet, she walked down the hall.

"Nancy, where are you going?" Heather was just coming up the back stairs.

"Miss Wade cornered me for another soul-searching talk.

She's waiting now. I'd give anything to get out of it, especially tonight."

"You poor kid." Heather's blue eyes darkened with sympathy for her friend. "I'll think of something, but you better get going now. Promptness, you know."

"I guess so. See you tomorrow. No doubt I'll be stuck with her till the lights-out bell."

Nancy was conflicted about Miss Wade. She wondered if Miss Hicks had put her up to all this religion talk or if she was for real. She had made some good points last time they talked, but still, she was over the top. Meeting with her once in a while would be okay with Nancy, but she'd much prefer to spend her free time with Heather.

Miss Wade's door was ajar. The invitation was obvious, but Nancy deliberately waited to be asked in after knocking.

"Enter." Miss Wade's voice betrayed her impatience at Nancy's formality. "Close the door and sit down. Not there, on the bed beside by me. How have you been getting along the past couple of weeks? It *has* been that long since we had our last talk, hasn't it?"

"Yes, Miss Wade, I'm afraid so." Nancy sat on the edge of the bed and glanced wistfully at the door.

"What do we have here, my dear?" Miss Wade cupped her hand under Nancy's chin, "have you been crying?" Nancy's hair fell away from her face, exposing her to the teacher's scrutiny.

"It's nothing, Miss Wade. I guess I was just feeling sad."

"You should have come to me sooner, Nancy. We know that you always feel so much better after our talks. It lifts your spirits to be with God."

"But I'm still trying to find Him," Nancy said, wanting nothing more than to appease Miss Wade and get out of there.

"Yes my dear, I know." Miss Wade's face lit with inspiration. "Perhaps you will find Him tonight."

"Nancy Walden. Telephone. Nancy Walden. Telephone."

Heather's voice resounded urgently from the telephone booth at the head of the back stairs.

Nancy stood and faced Miss Wade. "I want you to know that you have convinced me that I *will* find God," she said eagerly, "but as you so kindly and honestly taught me, it is something I can only do by myself."

"True my dear, but you will still need guidance." Miss Wade leaned forward as if to hold her captive there.

"Nancy Walden. Telephone."

"Please excuse me. The phone is for me. But thank you for everything, Miss Wade."

Oh Lord, she thought, as she ran down the hall, who would be calling her? Her mother? Philip? No, the only thing she could think was that it must be something to do with the baby. Her baby.

Miss Wade stared after Nancy. She was overwhelmed by feelings of desertion, and loneliness swept through her. She lay back and shut her eyes.

Miss Wade's spiritual sensitivity recognized a change in Nancy's attitude. The child was resisting her. It had to be that Brock girl that had latched onto Nancy. Heather Brock has influenced my protégé and might poison her against me...and God.

"Oh God," she declared, "I will save her from that girl. I promise I will bring Nancy Walden back to serve You. Her selflessness will be as strong as mine!"

Miss Wade turned on her side, and drew her legs toward her chest arranging herself in the fetal position. She felt dizzy. So dizzy. She was thankful to be lying down. The familiar warmth spread from her groin through her body and she welcomed the heavenly pain. God was near.

These hot flashes were her cross to bear for serving God in faith and constancy. She didn't mind them because they were the sign that she was connected to God. That was her unshakable perception. She wiped her moist brow.

Miss Wade rested for a moment longer then heaved herself off the bed and walked into her bathroom to shower.

Nancy left Miss Wade's room and rushed to the telephone booth. Pulling the door open, she was amazed to find Heather huddled on the floor, shaking with laughter. She waved her hand frantically at Nancy to come in and then picked up the receiver. "Quick, pretend you're talking," she whispered folding herself up to make room for Nancy.

Understanding the ruse at last, Nancy squeezed into the booth, picked up the phone and said; "Hello God. What can I do for you? Do I hear you correctly? You want me to tell Miss Wade to fly a kite? Well, I don't approve, but it is my duty to do your will. By the way, God, before you hang up, I think Heather should be blessed for rescuing me tonight."

Nancy's voice broke as she replaced the receiver on the hook. The two girls ran from the phone booth to Heather's room, their sides aching from the effort to control their laughter.

"That was the greatest mercy mission you may ever perform," Nancy said, grinning. "I thought I was hooked for sure."

"A friend in need..." Heather replied with a radiant smile.

"You are a friend, Heather. I can't tell you how much it means to me."

"Why are the girls so vicious? They enjoy dragging people down."

The radiance faded from Heather's face. Her chin dropped toward her chest.

"I don't know why, Nancy. Nothing better to do, I guess."

"That's a poor excuse for casually ruining someone's reputation."

"*Sometimes* the girls are sensitive to other people's feelings. I guess it depends on who it is."

A pulse in Nancy's neck throbbed as she scrutinized Heather. Was there a hidden meaning in her statement, an innuendo about Nancy's circumstances?

The bell rang its curfew message. Nancy moved toward the door and waved goodnight, determined to ignore her misgivings.

Neither friend could sleep that night. Nancy couldn't because she feared that her secret might be common knowledge and Heather because she felt compelled to tell Nancy what the girls were saying about her.

Good Lord, Nancy thought, What if everyone knew about her baby? If the whole school knew, she might as well just die.

At three-thirty in the morning, driven by her anxiety to hear the truth, Nancy quietly slipped out of bed and tiptoed across the room. She held her breath as she pressed her ear against the door, hearing every creak and gust of wind. Trembling, she stepped into the hall and tapped on Heather's door, whispering, "Heather, are you awake? "

"Yes, come on in. I couldn't sleep either. "I was just wishing for someone to talk to. We'll have to be real quiet, that's all. You know what they say about Waddles, how she sleeps with one ear glued to her door."

Heather rolled over toward the edge of her bed, and Nancy curled up under the other end of her quilt.

"You know, I was thinking that I was hard on the girls tonight," Nancy said nonchalantly. "Because there are some things like that wild story about Miss Hicks, that are pretty juicy tidbits. I'm sure that Miss Hicks couldn't care less what the girls say about her."

Nancy wished she could see Heather's face so she could detect her reaction.

Goose bumps ran up Heather's spine.

Nancy was putting their friendship to a supreme test. She suspected that people thought she had had a baby. *Did she want the truth or simple assurance that her fears were unwarranted?*

Heather forced herself to meet Nancy's eyes. "They think you had a baby."

"No. Oh no! Everyone knows?"

"Nancy, you've got to try to rise above it all. I mean not one of those girls is worth your little finger. Please don't cry."

How could she face anyone now? No wonder Sheila said that about Miss Hicks. It had really been aimed at her.

Nancy stood up and started toward the door. She didn't want to talk about this. Not now. Not ever.

"Please don't go, Nancy, please stay and talk." Heather grabbed Nancy's arm. "Talk to me. I don't judge you. I only want to comfort you. You're my best friend ever, and I want to be here for you."

Nancy stood in the middle of the room and pulled the heavy quilt tight around her petite frame. Humiliated, she struck out at Heather. "Don't worry. I'm not going to kill myself. If I had courage, I would have done it long ago."

"Oh Nance, I feel as though I've let you down."

Sorry for her harsh words, Nancy whispered, "No Heather, you're the only friend I have." Her voice broke and she dove back onto the end of Heather's bed and buried her head beneath the quilt. "Lord," she mumbled, "I hate my mother."

"What?"

"I said that I hate my mother," Nancy told her, "It's her fault that this story got around." It hurt so much to talk about this.

"See, I told the girls that it was a lie," Heather said.

"That's just the trouble, Heather, it isn't a lie, it's true. God forgive me, it's true. But my mother didn't have to tell Miss Hicks. There are plenty of reasons for a girl to transfer in the middle of the year. The minute one person knows, the whole world might as well know. There's no such thing as confidence."

"That's not so, Nancy. Look at us. I haven't mentioned

that letter deal, and neither have you. That is something we just know. I have confidence in our friendship."

Nancy sniffled. "That's true I suppose, but I really feel like I've been sold down river. By my mother and Miss Hicks. And everyone else who has repeated the story, for that matter."

"Your mother probably couldn't avoid telling Miss Hicks."

"You don't know my mother. She could avoid a third world war if she wanted to. It's because of her that I'm stuck here at Winthrop Academy while my baby is God-knows-where. To say nothing of Philip..." Nancy's voice drifted off.

"Then you did have a baby?" Heather asked softly.

"Yes, I did, Heather."

Absolute silence pervaded the room.

"You think I'm terrible, don't you?" Nancy said. "I sound like a character right out of *Peyton Place*."

Clutching the quilt, she leaned against the wall and stared into the darkness.

Heather did not hesitate. "No, I certainly do not," she said. "But at least your mother stuck by you and that's more than you can say for most parents."

"Ha! What a laugh," Nancy replied. "She stuck by me all right. She didn't let me out of her sight till I left for the home in Boston. She wouldn't let Philip come to the house or call." Her voice lowered to a whisper. "He didn't even try after a while. It was so obvious how he felt, the way he avoided me in school. He just dropped out of my life. My mother was afraid I might say something indiscreet that would get back to her friends. She let me know that my sister Joannie would never have disgraced her the way I did. But the point is, if she had really been concerned about my happiness, she would have let me marry Philip," Nancy said. "I actually thought about killing her! Isn't that horrible?"

"No, that's not horrible, Nancy. You must have gone through hell."

A sigh escaped her lips.

"Do you still love Philip?"

"Are you kidding? No. Too much has happened. It's just fantastic how one little moment can change your whole life."

"You poor kid."

Nancy knew she would never forget the day it happened. Philip's mother was out shopping and they were studying together on Philip's sun porch. It was a beautiful early spring day. They started tickling each other and he pinned her on her back. She was laughing hysterically. He kissed her then and her lips began to tingle. She thought of love, how forever it was. She could feel his body pressing against hers, his hands trembling as he reached under her sweater. So this is what it was, wanting something you're not supposed to want. "We shouldn't," she breathed into his shoulder. But by then, she didn't mean it.

Then they were kissing again and he was calling her name as if in pain. She was breathing so hard it made her dizzy. It wasn't premeditated. It had just happened, as innocently as that. It was like a dream. There was no reality. Until afterwards.

"Did you keep on doing it after that?"

"Lord, no. We were scared to death at what we had done and swore to each other that we would never do it again until we were married. But of course the damage was done."

Well, sixteen is really young, you know, even if you are in love."

"I know sixteen was too young," Nancy flared. "We certainly didn't plan it that way."

"I'm sure you didn't. All I'm saying is that hating your mother won't erase what happened. You might be blaming her when actually you hate yourself."

"That makes sense in a way, 'cause I do torture myself over having gotten pregnant. It was so stupid. I should have known better. But, Lord, I hardly knew what sex was all about. You'll laugh, but you know something? I still don't, really."

"Me, too. Hey, we should sign up with Jennifer for private tutoring on the subject"

Nancy laughed for the first time. "Yes. Jennifer is quite a powerhouse, isn't she? But as you said before, who knows what is fact and what is fantasy."

The girls sat in agreement in the darkness. "Nancy, what do

you feel the most guilt about?" There was urgency in Heather's question.

"It's the baby," Nancy answered without even pausing. "My baby is what I agonize over. The poor little thing that never asked to be born. The baby I dumped out into the world as though I didn't care what anyone did with it. Oh, if only mother hadn't made me give her up."

Nancy's throat tightened, choking off the rest of her sentence.

"But don't you see that what you did was best for the baby?"

Heather sat up, slung her arm around Nancy's shoulder and dipped her head so she could look directly at her. "Imagine having a seventeen-year-old for a mother," she said. "Instead, you've made some married couple happy and provided the best possible future for your baby."

"I know you are right logically," Nancy told her, "but sometimes I wake up in the silence to the sound of a baby crying. And it breaks my heart. I went through so much and have nothing to show for it."

"You can't keep thinking about it or you'll send yourself to the nut house," Heather said.

"I know. That's what I was doing when I first came here with no one to talk to. You're the Ann Landers of Winthrop Academy, Heather. I'm thankful that you're my friend." Nancy smiled shyly in the dark.

"I couldn't agree more."

"But Heather, how can I face the girls?"

"I'll tell you how," Heather interrupted angrily, "you'll never let on that you're aware of their suspicions."

"But what if someone asks or it comes out in the open?"

"Then you will deny it or laugh it off. I doubt if half the girls believe what they are blabbing about. It's just another way to pass the time. Don't take what they say personally, like tonight. As a matter of fact, make a few cracks of your own."

Nancy realized that dawn must be breaking because she could see the outline of Heather's face. "Good grief," she said, "its morning. I've got to get out of here before Jennifer wakes up. Or Miss Wade. Thanks for everything, Heather."

Folding the quilt over the arm of a chair, she slipped quietly from the room, thankful for the gift of friendship. Nothing could take that away.

CHAPTER SIX

Sheila was depressed. Friday mail call had not produced her regular laundry case filled with the expected homemade yummies. She hated it when her mother didn't mail the case on time, particularly when she was as hungry as she had been lately. It also upset Sheila to realize that no one bothered to stop by her room, as was the Friday night custom. She wandered down to the smoking lounge and collapsed into a chair apart from the group.

"God, is it ever boring around here," Jennifer complained. She sucked at her Lucky Strike and pursed her lips to form a perfect smoke ring. The girls watched the ring as it drifted away.

"Where's Nancy?" Karen asked.

"Wherever Heather is, naturally, where else?" Jennifer snapped.

"That's a bummer," Sheila chimed in.

Jennifer shrugged. Her roommate never spent any of her free time with her. "She's a real drag, anyway."

"Nancy is quiet, but I think she's sweet," Karen said.

"Shut up, you kids. Here they come." Audrey stood near the open door and it gave her a full view of the back stairwell.

Nancy and Heather strolled into the lounge laughing at something, oblivious of the fact that every eye in the room was on them.

"Hi kids," Karen said sliding a chair toward Heather with her foot.

Nancy lit a Kool, drew the smoke deep into her lungs and flopped onto the couch next to Karen.

"I don't know about you guys," Sheila said, "but I'm starved. If my laundry case had arrived today, we'd be indulging ourselves right now."

"It's too bad 'cause we really look forward to those Friday night sessions in your room," Karen replied with so little conviction that even Sheila didn't know if she meant it.

Jennifer jumped to her feet and began pacing around the room. "Gads, it's like a morgue around here."

"Let's do something wicked," Sheila suggested.

"Like what?" Audrey asked, still leaning against the door jam.

The room fell silent. It was as though they had become a planning committee with Sheila in charge.

"I've got it!" Sheila shouted, suddenly elated. "Let's raid the kitchen."

"That's a great idea."

"Anything to break the monotony."

Nancy looked questioningly at Heather who shrugged.

"Okay it's agreed," Sheila said. "Now we must decide when and how? This is going to be the greatest. Let's meet in the bathroom at twelve-thirty tonight. Waddles ought to be asleep by then. After that we'll go down the back stairs, through the outside passage-way and hit the lockers near the back of the kitchen."

Jennifer looked sharply at Sheila. "Say, it sounds like you've done this before. You hot shit. I bet you're the mystery raider."

Sheila denied it.

"Methinks the lady doth protest too much," Karen said, grinning.

"Oh, Christ. There goes the warning bell."

"Come on you guys; let's be model tonight. Maybe Waddles will crap out early."

"Wear socks," Sheila told them, "it's quieter that way. Oh, and be sure to bring your pillow cases for the loot."

At twelve-fifteen that night, Sheila's alarm clock which she had buried beneath her pillow, buzzed. Waking with a start, she pressed every button until she found the right one.

As in Sheila's case, most of the girls idled in bed wondering, as the initial enthusiasm for the prank had passed, would anyone really be waiting in the bathroom? Because no one wanted to be a party pooper, one girl after the other shook her pillow from its case, and crept out of her room. Morale rose considerably when all six of them converged in the bathroom.

"Come on you guys, let's go," Sheila whispered. "Be quiet. Go single file. And for goodness sake watch out where you walk."

Clutching her pillowcase, Sheila stuck her head around the corner, and strained her ear toward the long tomblike hall leading to Miss Wade's closed door. Satisfied, she shuffled to the head of the stairs, and signaled over her shoulder for the girls to follow.

The flannel-clad gang of thieves crept down the stairs. Six shadowy forms rocking from side to side as they stepped on the edges of the stairs to avoid any squeaks.

Downstairs, in the pitch dark hallway, they formed a tight little group. The passage was freezing cold, but it led to the kitchen.

"If there are any cowards here," Jennifer hissed, "now's the time to quit."

A moment of silence prevailed while each girl listened for someone else to chicken out.

"Let's cut the crap and move on, my feet are frozen," Audrey whispered.

"Yes, let's go before we lose our nerve," Nancy agreed.

"We've already lost our heads," Heather commented.

Karen giggled. "At least we are all in this together."

"To the Corridor Girls!" Jennifer saluted them.

"Stop that stupid tee-heeing," Sheila scolded. "The success of this deal depends on absolute quiet. Now follow me." The wintry chill of the unheated passageway made them shiver.

"Wait a minute," Heather warned, "I hear something."

The girls came to a standstill, each strained to hear.

"What if it's The Creep?"

"I don't smell anything, so it can't be him."

"Come on, let's keep going."

They moved forward.

"My teeth are chattering." Nancy shivered and moved closer to Heather for warmth.

Karen tapped Jennifer's shoulder. "Pass the word to Sheila that I've got to go to the bathroom." The message went no further than Jennifer who stopped so abruptly that Karen bumped into her.

"For Pete's sakes, you should've taken a leak before we started out," Jennifer snapped.

"Jeez, you guys," Sheila said. "This is like Halloween. What're you doing back there, building a pyramid? I was just about to go in. Now will you untangle yourselves and shut up?"

It was Sheila who opened the door to the kitchen with its welcoming night-light. Just then, Nancy sneezed. The girls froze, straining to hear if they had been caught.

"No more of that or I'll have a heart attack," Audrey warned.

With a flourish of bravado, Jennifer broke from the group. "Come on you blundering idiots," she said, "let's get at the goods."

As a single body, they advanced toward the food lockers.

"Jesus H. Christ, Sheila," Jennifer hissed, "you goofed. The damn door is locked."

Sheila responded with a mysterious smile and signaled them to calm down. Opening the dishwasher, she reached deep inside and extracted a key that she dangled in front of their amazed faces.

"I saw Mabel hide it in there when I was cutting through the kitchen months ago," she explained.

"You're an unending source of information," Nancy marveled while the others murmured in agreement. Sheila grinned.

"Let's get on with it or my bladder's going to burst," Karen whispered.

Sheila opened the locker door, managing to knock a pan from the wall in the process. It clattered to the floor, and resounded loudly. Panic ensued.

"Now we've had it."

"Why don't you watch out, you idiot?"

"I'm going to wet my pants."

"I'm scared."

"Get your clammy hands off me."

"What'll we do?"

"Shut the damn door."

Except for the pounding of her heart, Sheila heard nothing but she still held up her arms for silence. Two minutes passed like hours.

"What in heaven's name is that?" Jennifer's voice broke the silence.

"What?" Heather asked. "Oh my gosh, what is it?"

"Yuk. Who spilled something?" Audrey demanded.

Karen tittered.

"Oh Karen, you didn't!" Nancy exclaimed.

"Good gravy," Jennifer said, "Karen peed her pants."

"I couldn't hold it any longer." Karen's voice sounded very faint, but then she began giggling again. Someone else snickered. Soon it became contagious and the girls burst into hysterical laughter.

"Oooo my sides ache..."

"My face hurts from laughing..."

Gasping for breath, Sheila turned on the light. "Well now that Karen feels better, let's scoff the eats and get the hell out of here before anything else happens."

Karen found paper towels and diligently mopped up her mess.

"Maybe if we're not pigs about it they won't miss anything," Nancy said to Sheila whose pillowcase was already half filled with various cans and boxes.

"Yes," Heather agreed, "we should only take what we can eat in one session."

"Okay. Okay," Jennifer said impatiently. "Let's bomb out of here. I'm starting to get twitchy, cooped up in this locker with all you queers."

They hesitated for a moment after Sheila replaced the key. No one was looking forward to the journey back. "Come on," Audrey urged them, "let's get brave you guys."

The return was far more rapid than their descent due to pure relief that the expedition was almost over. By the time Sheila led them to the end of the passageway, they disregarded caution completely. The girls ran, bumped into each other, pushed and gasped in their haste to be back in the safety of their rooms.

Nancy took the stairs two at a time, caring less about squeaks and creaks this time.

"Let's meet for a banquet tomorrow night, okay, guys?"

They all heard Sheila's stage whisper but no one answered.

"Phew, what a hairy piece of action that was," Jennifer said to Nancy as she dove onto her bed.

"You can say that again," Nancy answered.

Sheila closed her bedroom door behind her and climbed under her covers, smiling to herself. Even though she guessed that the girls hadn't delighted in their nocturnal excursion that much, she knew that it would become part of the school's mythology and that she would be remembered as the instigator of their adventure.

The next day, the corridor girls seemed to avoid one another as they occupied themselves with the usual Saturday tasks. At ten in the morning, the whole school gathered in the reception hall for Glee Club practice. Even if she couldn't carry a tune in a paper bag, every girl was required to participate, although a few were told not to sing, just to make their mouths move. It had to do with school spirit.

After dinner that night when the girls congregated in the smoking lounge, an air of secret anticipation prevailed.

"Well ladies, do you really think we got away with it?" Sheila said, digging in her pockets for her cigarettes. She noted that there were no old candy bars, not even a box of jujubes.

"Naturally," Audrey replied with her usual disdain. "If they knew, you can be sure that we would have heard about it by now."

"Maybe they're just being foxy," Heather suggested.

"Will you guys relax?" Jennifer said. "We pulled it off like professionals."

"Well, it's all over now but the eating," Karen rationalized. "Besides I think it was exciting."

"That was obvious," Jennifer teased, "you were so excited that you couldn't control yourself." The girls laughed uproariously.

"It was the best fun I've had in ages," Sheila exclaimed. "Let's skip the movie and get started now."

"What are they showing tonight?" Karen asked.

"*Great Expectations*," the girls answered in unison.

"Good God," Jennifer said. "They'd have better attendance if they showed *Around the World in Eighty Days* or *Sweet Smell of Success*. Oh, that Burt Lancaster is so sexy."

"What happened to Elvis, Jennifer?" Sheila demanded.

"He's sexy, too."

"Anyway, it's not like Miss Hicks could get hold of a flick that just came out. Besides, she says that the classics broaden our minds. Or some such shit. Let's forget the movies and dig in. It's going to take us half the night to eat all that stuff."

Stubbing out their cigarettes, the girls followed Sheila to her room, where, without ceremony, they emptied their pillowcases onto Sheila's bed. And the feast began.

❧

Sunday dinner was uneventful. Afterwards, Nancy and Heather decided to bundle up and battle the elements. Jennifer went directly to her room to prepare for the rendezvous with Jonathan Herrick. The corridor was empty.

It was hard to believe that this was the first day of March, Jennifer thought, watching gusts of wind waft the powdery snow into cone-shaped swirls that drifted across the field outside her window. Groups of girls walked with heads bent against the wind, apparently invigorated by the bitter cold. Jennifer was sorry that she had ever hinted that anything was going on between her and Jonathan. She was determined to be quiet about it now that she had captured him. She had never anticipated that this sexual adventure would last this long.

Jennifer had prepared herself as carefully as though she were a bride. After her shower, she examined herself in the bathroom mirror. The knowledge that he was attracted to her made her glow inside. Could there be more to their relationship? Probably he thought she was a dumb jerk with hot pants. Sure she liked sex. What's so bad about that? But why shouldn't they have a meeting of minds, too? She wondered if he had noticed her before her blatant attempts to get his attention. Had he also noticed that she had a straight "A" average and made articulate comments when she spoke in class? *Was love possible?*

She thought it was more satisfying being with an older man, a single, worldlier man who loved sex as much as she did, but who respected her, too. Jonathan was not like the boys back home who would say or do anything to get you in the back seat of a car.

Jennifer padded back to her room to dress, still deep in thought.

Jonathan really wasn't so bad looking, especially when he took his glasses off. He seemed vulnerable then. At least she could feel secure with a man who would adore her completely, and Jonathan would be grateful he had someone like her. He was a man who wouldn't be chased by every horny girl around.

She wondered if Jonathan could love her. He wouldn't be like Doctor Daddy, who screwed every patient that came into his office. Her father was so handsome, but he was such a rat. She wondered if he ever hated himself. Jennifer would have felt sorry for Mumsie except that she knew that she had her own distractions.

Oh hell, now I'm getting ahead of myself. Jennifer inspected the finished product thoroughly before she dabbed perfume on her wrists and behind her ears as a final touch. She expected that Jonathan Herrick was as anxious for her to arrive as she was. Their encounter in the volleyball closet had been exciting although too quick. What would it be like when they were really alone and leisurely?

She decided to stroll beyond the driveway, and then cut through the woods to the back of his cottage, certain that no one could see her from the school. She wondered what his place was like. Well, it wouldn't be long before she would see for herself.

After a little deliberation, Jonathan Herrick decided that his absence from Sunday dinner would not be considered odd as he had a habit of occasionally skipping meals, especially when there was inclement weather. But what if Jennifer didn't show up because of the storm? No, he assured himself, it would take more than bad weather to deter Jennifer from doing whatever she wanted. He grinned. She wanted him badly enough to wade through a little snow.

She was so beautiful. Young boys by the score must be chasing after her, so why him? He would be the first to admit that he was no prize package. Yet, if she only craved sex, then the fact that Jake and Dave were married teachers wouldn't make any difference. So, he reasoned, there must be more depth to her feelings for him. Maybe her flippant attitude was merely a cover-up.

God, what if she was in love with him?

But he mustn't think like that. It would be dangerous to become too emotionally involved.

He looked around the living room with its heavy gold drapes, a burgundy leather chair and matching couch, and a gold shag rug covering most of the floor. He rearranged the coals in the fireplace and watched the flames grow stronger. The unmarried female teachers had apartments in the main building. Thank goodness he had this privacy.

He opened the bedroom door, and stood back to verify that his picture in full Air Force uniform was visible from the living room. Uh oh! Beside the framed photograph, the desk was littered with model airplanes in various stages of completion. *What if she laughed at that?* With sudden fear of humiliation, he rushed to the bathroom for a towel and draped it over the table to hide his hobby from view. Then as a final touch, he shut the bedroom door.

Back in the kitchen, Jonathan took a bottle of Scotch out of the cupboard where it had been sitting untouched since the beginning of the term and took a gulp to quiet his nerves.

He closed the drapes in the living room and was sitting by the fireside, trying to concentrate on reading Edwin O'Connor's *The Last Hurrah*, when there was a knock at the back door. He had expected to greet her at the front door, and his courage faded in the face of Jennifer's unpredictability. He dashed into the kitchen.

"Hi," Jennifer said, already shrugging off her L.L. Bean Academy parka and handing it to him as unselfconsciously as though she were a daily visitor.

Jonathan placed it over the back of a chair, and felt a thrill when he watched her pat her hair. Already his heart was beating unevenly. He slid his hands around her waist and bent to bury his face in her thick chestnut hair. She stood on tiptoe caressing his cheek with her lips before pulling away and scooting past him into the living room.

"Let's see what the rest of the pad looks like," she called back over her shoulder. "Wow! This room is really neato. And look at that fabulous fireplace. It was worth braving the storm just for this."

She kicked off her shoes and shuffled like a child through the thick shag carpet, then lowered herself to the floor and propped her head on her hand to stare into the flames. She wore a matching cashmere skirt and sweater in a soft yellow that blended into the gold of the carpet.

All this while, Jonathan stood in the doorway, delighted by Jennifer's enthusiasm. She was child-like one moment, the next, womanly and worldly. He had never been interested in a student before, but God, she drove him to distraction. He gazed at her skirt, pulled tight around that pert little bottom. In an attempt to hide his excitement, he retreated to the kitchen to pour two cokes, adding a shot of Scotch to his glass.

Jennifer was still gazing at the fire's embers. She heard him return, and rolled onto her back with her hands behind her head, her hair flowing out over the rug. Her eyes were closed.

Jonathan stood over her, wearing an unguarded expression of longing. He placed the drinks and his glasses on the hearth, and then stretched out beside her. She was magnetic. He couldn't resist her. But dammit, he thought, I'm the master of this ship and I'll be aggressive when I feel like it.

"How about a coke?" he asked.

"Not now, thanks."

He drained his glass in three long gulps and then turned on his side. His eyes ravished her face and body.

"When we were in the gym, you said that you couldn't get pregnant?" his voice faded into a question.

She sat up to contemplate her answer. If she told him she took the pills to rectify an irregular period, he might not believe her. Besides, she didn't want to lie to him. But what would he think of the truth?

"I take contraceptive pills," she said, turning to look at him. "My dad's a doctor and I got them from his salesman's supply. It's such a new idea. They're not even officially on the market yet. Of course Europeans are using them already."

Her manner was brisk, matter-of-fact. She reached across him for a cigarette from the open pack on the coffee table.

Jonathan took the lighter from her and watched her face as she took a deep drag on the cigarette. "How come?" he asked.

"How come what?"

"How come you take those pills?"

"My parents were afraid their wild daughter might do something to humiliate them, so they figured an ounce of prevention wouldn't hurt anyone."

"You're a different person than you were at the beginning of the school year," he told her. "Do you realize how you've changed?"

"Well, I must admit that I like myself a little better now than I did before. But I have you to thank for that, don't I?"

He took her in his arms and kissed her gently on the forehead.

"You're very beautiful," he said quietly.

"I know."

"Are you happy?"

"Now? Yes."

He placed his hand on her breast, moving it gently in circular motions until he could feel her nipples harden under the thin protection of her sweater.

"Do I make you happy?" he asked.

"You can."

"Can any one else?"

"Why don't you undress me?"

"Why don't you wear a brassiere?" he asked, unbuttoning the front of her cardigan, entranced by the youthful firmness of her breasts.

"Do you want me to?"

"It's just that I thought that all girls did."

He tossed her clothes on the couch and ran his hands possessively over her body. It was wonderful to have privacy and time.

How defenseless she seemed in her nakedness.

He discarded his own clothing without embarrassment. "I want you..." He broke off as though the very potency of his desire was choking him.

No one had ever looked at Jennifer like that. There was a powerful need boiling between them, a need they both knew was mutual.

Aroused by his passion, she pressed her cheek against

his matted chest. She whispered, "Take me to bed, Jonathan. Now."

Scooping her up in his arms, he felt that nothing was insurmountable. She relaxed in his arms.

Jonathan placed her on the bed as if she were a porcelain doll.

His fingers worked their magic until her body trembled. He explored her mouth with his tongue. She disappeared into the depth of his kiss.

Jennifer gave herself without reservation to his lovemaking and he in turn, responded to her embraces with an ardor he never dreamed he possessed.

She threw her leg over his thigh and pressed herself hard against him. He felt the muscles in his groin tighten. Passion pounded at his temples when she opened her legs to receive him, locking them possessively around his back. He thrust himself into her over and over until they both climaxed.

They remained in silent comfort, his arm around her, her leg across his. Time slowed, and neither knew how long they lay together.

"Cigarette?"

"Mmmm. Oh, you smoke Luckies, too! That has to mean something. "

In the quiet, they smoked, feeling the tender affection that came from having taken and given wholly of one's self.

Cigarettes smoked to a butt, perspiration cooled to a chill, each waited for the other to speak...to set the tone.

"Are you cold?"

"Yes, a little."

Jonathan pulled the sheet and blanket up and smoothed them tenderly over her. As he turned on his side, he looked deep into her velvet-brown eyes as though he could absorb her thoughts by merely looking. He kissed her gently.

"So this is what a man's bedroom looks like?" she asked him, demure now, tucking the sheet around herself as she pushed back against the headboard.

"You've never been in one before?"

"Not for this reason."

"Where did you get all your experience?" he asked, immediately sorry for his peevish tone.

"In the back of cars," she answered flippantly. "But actually..." she turned to look at him squarely.

"Actually what?" he prompted.

"Actually, I'm full of hot air." She looked away from him, clearly embarrassed.

"I love you for that," he said, and enfolded her in his arms.

"Why?" she asked as she pressed her face against his shoulder.

"Because I think you're trying to be honest with me, and I appreciate it."

"It doesn't come easy, believe me. I bet you never lie."

"Only if my life depends on it. Or my job."

"Like maybe never. Hey, that isn't you, is it? Were you really in the Air Force?"

"Oh that," he laughed in an attempt to disparage his success. "I was one of those fly boys."

"Do you still fly?"

"Well, I haven't been up in almost a year now, but it wouldn't take much to get with it again."

"Would you take me for a ride? Would you, Jonathan?"

He chuckled and hugged her. "Of course I would. Maybe this summer..."

They exchanged a startled look, each fearful of the future, each preferring to remain in the security of here and now.

"How about that coke now," he said, breaking the unwelcome tension.

"Great idea. I'm really dry after all that huffing and puffing."

Her thoughts drifted to his comment about this summer. Immediately she pictured them in their own apartment, grocery shopping together, living together next fall. As long as she attended college, her parents would be thrilled not to have to deal with her any more.

He slid out of bed, and disappeared from the room. Without

warning, her clothes landed on top of her as he called from the doorway; "Let's get dressed and visit in front of the fire." He closed the door, leaving Jennifer alone.

While dressing, she examined everything in the room, not feeling the least bit nosy or presumptuous. Look at these models, she thought peering under the towel, that's kind of cute...like a kid.

Her clothes on and hair in place, she returned to the living room where shortly after, he joined her with refreshments that they ate in silence as they sat together on the rug.

Gazing into the yellow-orange embers of the fire, she sighed in contentment. "What time is it, anyway?"

"Five-twenty."

"Oh my God, I've been here over three hours," she yelped with alarm, jumping to her feet. "If I don't run all the way, I'll miss dinner. And Miss Hicks will know. I'm at her table this week."

She rushed to the kitchen for her coat, Jonathan followed closely behind.

"Here, let me help you. I can hardly believe the time went by so quickly. My dear Jennifer, when can it be again?"

"How about next Sunday?" she suggested, grasping the back doorknob.

"Why not Saturday, too?"

He tried to embrace her once more, but she darted out the door, leaving him shivering in the snow-filled air.

CHAPTER SEVEN

"I don't know why, but rainy Sundays are the worst," Nancy said as she stood by the window in Heather's room. "They're so depressing."

"At least it's better than snow," Heather replied. She was lying across the end of her bed throwing her stuffed kitten in the air and catching it.

The only sound inside the room was the snap of electricity as Nancy ran the brush in lazy strokes through her long hair. Lost in thought, she continued to gaze at the rain drumming down onto the dirt-crusted snow.

"Your hair is so shiny," Heather told her. "I wish mine weren't so darn curly. I'd grow it long like yours."

"Philip used to say how feminine it was."

"Boy, you seem down in the dumps." Heather stood up and stretched. "Let's get back to the books. Exams make me a nervous wreck...three hours long. That's as bad as college prelims are supposed to be."

They both jumped when the door burst open and Sheila appeared waving a slip of paper. "Hey, you guys, did you see this notice on the main bulletin board? Quick, come on into my room. Round up the rest of the kids and I'll meet you there." Then she was gone.

"What do you imagine that was all about?" Nancy asked.

"Beats me, but we might as well go find out."

As they stepped into the hall, Nancy saw Jennifer and Audrey heading the same way each wearing quizzical expressions.

"Well, it's all a matter of conscience," Karen was saying to Sheila as they entered the room. As soon as they were all together, Sheila read aloud: ***The girl or girls responsible, or in any way involved in last Friday's escapade, please see Miss Hicks in her office Tuesday, immediately after dinner.***

"Why did they wait so long?" Karen demanded.

Audrey smirked, "Obviously they were having midnight meetings first to decide what they would do with the culprits."

"Lord, you don't think we'll be expelled, do you?" Nancy asked, her brown eyes wide as she considered the possibility.

"Imagine being kicked out for such a stupid reason," Sheila exclaimed. "Miss Hicks says we're supposed to feel like home here, and yet we can't eat when we want to...not in our lounge, not between meals."

"The only reasons for expulsion that I know of are cheating, leaving campus without permission, smoking outside the lounge, or stealing," Karen reassured her.

"You'd think they caught us red-handed, the way you're all carrying on," Audrey sneered. "Relax air-heads. We got away with it and they'll never know who it was. Unless one of us rats on the rest." She glared at each girl in turn.

Heather stood up. Nancy knew that whatever she said would be fair and level headed. "We were all involved in this deal," she said with authority. "So whatever we feel is best to do as a group, everyone will have to abide by the decision."

"Okay," Sheila said laughing. "So let's make up our minds right now that we'll keep quiet about it."

Sheila the quick-fix girl. Nancy had expected more from her.

"It's not going to be as easy as that, Sheila," Heather said. "There's a little matter of truth."

"Oh please," Jennifer retorted, "don't give us that crap, Heather. You're talking about confession. I say, what they don't know won't hurt them."

Jennifer's response didn't surprise Nancy either, although lately, she had seemed to be kinder, less sarcastic.

Sheila kicked her closet door shut. "Good heavens, we only took a little food. Was that so bad? After all, they would have given it to us eventually anyway."

"Yeah," Audrey agreed. "What's a little food?"

"I just had a thought," Karen said. "What if they decide to punish the whole school if no one confesses?"

Nancy had been thinking the same thing.

"Boy, that's just like the kind of dirty trick they'd play." For the first time, Sheila sounded worried.

"What's the worst they could do to us?" Audrey demanded. "Suspend us for a week? That would be more trouble for them than it's worth since they'd have to give us all make-up classes."

Nancy knew that Audrey's argument was making sense to the girls. It certainly did to her.

"That's true. It's not as though it was just one person that they could make a big example of," Nancy pointed out. "There's safety in numbers, so I vote for a mass confession."

"Me, too."

"I guess you're right."

"Count me in."

All eyes were on Jennifer who finally shrugged and rolled her eyes toward the ceiling. "Well, if you can't beat 'em, join 'em," she said.

"Hey, is that a Miss Hicks quote?"

Honestly, Sheila, Nancy thought, you're too much for movies.

❧

Miss Hicks lowered herself wearily into the chair behind her desk. She massaged both temples, hoping to delay the migraine that was threatening to plague her. At least they had showed her the courtesy of respecting her request to surrender themselves.

It was clear, however, that Sam, who was raising her eyebrows like crazy, was aggravated at her attitude. "I suppose the very fact that they took the food in the first place couldn't possibly indicate a lack of respect for your original request that they *not* do it," she said now. "Good heavens, Beth, don't delude yourself. Those kids did it and they're glad."

"I don't believe they were *all* glad," Miss Wade interrupted her, thinking of Nancy, but also feeling responsible because they were *her* girls, from *her* corridor.

"Glad or sorry is irrelevant at this point," Sam snapped. "What concerns us now is what to do about it."

"I know, I know."

The three maiden ladies contemplated a solution.

Miss Wade shifted her heavy legs to a more comfortable position and cleared her throat for attention, a habit for which Miss Hicks knew Sam nourished an intense dislike. "I think perhaps we should seek out the instigator and use her as an example that we do not intend to tolerate such flagrant disregard for authority. I say we should expel her. That would certainly put a stop to pranks like this."

At the thought, Miss Hicks' headache intensified.

"You said it, Gertrude. Only there's one fallacy. Those girls stick together like peas in a pod. It's the all-for-one motto. So you could never point your finger at just one girl."

"I'm not pointing any fingers, Sam," Miss Wade retorted in her own defense, taking a scone from the delicate plate on the small fluted table around which they were sitting. "I was simply trying to help find a means of putting an end to such disrespect. If the girls can't show reverence for man-made authority, how can they find it in their hearts to revere the Supreme Being and follow His laws?"

Suddenly, she felt her pulse quicken. She dropped the bite of scone onto the napkin in her lap and clenched her hands tightly, digging her nails into her palms. She simply could not have one of her hot flashes in front of her colleagues. She held her breath until the moment passed. Just the thought that she had received a message from God was enough to buoy her spirits and strengthen her convictions.

Sam smiled slyly at Miss Hicks who was still rubbing her temples. "Why don't we have the punishment fit the crime?" she suggested, sniffing loudly. "Don't allow desserts, food packages from home, or any snacks in between meals."

"That certainly would be fitting," Miss Hicks conceded.

"But it would be difficult to enforce. No, I think we shall have to campus them till spring vacation. What do you think of that, Sam?"

"I guess it's the best you can do."

"Gertrude?"

"You aren't firm enough with the girls, Beth. But if you insist on that action, you should at least say campused indefinitely. That at least has a little more onus to it."

Sam stood up. Miss Hicks knew this meant that she considered the meeting over.

Miss Hicks reasoned with herself. What about babysitting? The Packers wouldn't appreciate having their babysitting service rescinded. Then there was the dance. I want every girl to participate in all school functions. So the dance would definitely not be included in the punishment either.

"Well," she concluded, "I guess it will be: *no food from home and campused indefinitely*."

"So be it." Hilda Sampson said with finality.

"And the interpretation of its meaning is up to us," Miss Hicks said directly to Miss Wade since Sam had already left the room.

The moment Miss Wade spotted Nancy, she said, "I'd like to see you in my sitting room immediately after evening study hall."

"But, Miss Wade, we're studying for exams..."

"I'll be waiting."

She turned abruptly, and walked down the corridor to her apartment. There, she spent the study period planning exams for her history classes and waiting. Nancy arrived on time.

"Come in, my dear. Sit there." Miss Wade cleared her throat and waved her hand toward the chair beside her. "Of course, you must know why I wanted to speak with you, tonight especially."

"I'm not exactly sure, Miss Wade."

Nancy was apprehensive as she watched the teacher meticulously arrange her fountain pens and pencils in neat order of size.

"If you think a moment, you'll realize that the foolish escapade in which you became involved, was not only thoughtless in regard to me, but also disrespectful to God," Miss Wade began. "He has many ways in which to test your readiness for acceptance in His grace once again. I am afraid that the company you choose to keep distracts you from your goal, your main purpose in life is to find God and reunite yourself."

"I want to apologize for myself and the other girls who were involved in the kitchen raid," Nancy said, her words tumbling over one another in her rush to put an end to Miss Wade's sermon. "I realize now that it reflected on you since you're in charge of us. We're truly sorry, Miss Wade."

"That is very sweet of you, my dear, but it is hardly my point. I am afraid that some of the girls in this corridor are leading you in the wrong direction. You are a follower, Nancy. There is nothing wrong in that, but it does behoove you to choose your company wisely."

"I have a mind of my own, Miss Wade," she said as defiantly as she dared, "and just because I made one mistake in my life doesn't mean that I am doomed."

"Certainly not. And I meant to give no offense by saying that you are a follower, which you are, because where would God be without His sheep to follow in His ways? God uses me to guide His little lambs who go astray."

Nancy's mind was racing. She realized that something was drastically wrong with this woman. Who did she think she was, telling her she was a follower? Nancy had been a cheerleader and on student council before she dropped out of school to have the baby. If anything, Joannie was the follower, not her. Waddles was way out in left field. She didn't know her at all.

"I am trying to understand, Miss Wade, why those people who said they loved me, were not there for me when I needed them the most."

With amazement, Nancy realized she was thinking not

only of Philip, but of her mother when she said that. But what she realized most clearly in that moment was that she was desperate for someone to love her without demands. Not like Miss Wade. Like Heather.

The truth hurts, Nancy thought with desolation. She always did what other people wanted. If that was being a follower, then yes, she was a follower, even though she wished that she had the courage of her own convictions, taking steps to make her own dreams come true.

Miss Wade watched the troubled girl stare into space, deep in thought and with a sudden rush of tenderness foreign to her nature, the teacher went to Nancy and patted her head in consolation.

"My dear, my dear," she crooned. "You mustn't feel depressed. You must give your entire self to God and then He will lead you."

"I can't." Won't was more like it.

Standing beside Nancy, Miss Wade cupped her hand under her chin, and raised her head until the resentful eyes met her own.

"You *can* and you *will*, Nancy. But you must have faith, first in yourself then in me, for I will show you the way to God. You cannot *use* God," Miss Wade continued as she ran her fingers through Nancy's hair. "Rather, you must cleanse your heart and open your soul to Him. Only when you belong to Him completely will you have peace. Oh, my dear Nancy, divorce yourself from these evil doers and devote your mind and soul to finding God through me. Your body is tarnished, but God does not demand perfection, just complete submission and belief."

Nancy wrenched her head away, twisting her hair in a skein and tucking it into the back of her sweater. She realized she had to say something to shut her up so that she could escape. "I'll try, Miss Wade," she murmured, rising.

"As I am God's instrument, I will give you the strength from my soul to yours. Give me your faith and I will show you the way."

Miss Wade's voice caught with emotion as her chest began

to heave. She clutched Nancy's hand, and chanted, "She is mine now and soon I shall deliver her to You. Oh God, I love you, I am Yours."

The moment the teacher touched her, Nancy realized that all this had gone too far. She saw that Miss Wade was staring at the ceiling with glazed eyes, her mouth slightly open, perspiration beading on her forehead and nose.

"Are you okay?" Nancy demanded. Miss Wade's weirdness really frightened her now. For some strange reason she was reminded of her mother's response when she had told her she was pregnant. Only this time, she would do what *she* wanted, not what someone else wanted her to do. Just because this woman was an authority figure didn't mean that everything she said was true or that all her advice was valid.

Miss Wade staggered to the couch. "Go, child, please go. I'm all right. It's just these spells I have now and then."

"Are you sure?" Nancy insisted. Miss Wade wasn't really ill in the ordinary sense. Somehow she knew that. But something was clearly very wrong.

"Yes, my dear. I'll lie here for a while and then shower and go to bed. Please don't mention this, it's nothing. You run along and we'll talk again soon."

Nancy stepped into the corridor and closed the door behind her, confused and more uncertain than ever.

What she had just seen and heard had seriously frightened her. What if Miss Wade really was one of those religious fanatics?

There was only one concrete fact in her life now and that was Heather's friendship. Heather liked her just as she was, without reservations. Nancy had never experienced total acceptance before, and she knew she would not let go of Heather for anyone or anything.

Nancy sat dejectedly in Heather's room. It was Sunday,

but the corridor seemed like a tomb. "Well, it could be worse," Heather said, "we could have been expelled."

"It's so confining," Nancy told her. "Now I understand why my mother used to complain when her car was on the blink. Even if she didn't have plans, she hated the idea of it not sitting in the garage just in case she wanted to go somewhere."

Heather jumped to her feet. "Hey, 'campused indefinitely' doesn't mean we can't go for a walk, does it?"

"Brilliant idea," Nancy said, "let's go."

The two friends rushed down the stairs, struggling into their coats as they went. Just as Heather reached for the door, it swung open to reveal Mr. Jones, hunched as usual, staring at them from under his wavy-brimmed hat. Startled, she jumped back with a small yelp.

"Oh, Mr. Jones, you surprised me. How are you today?"

"Hello Mr. Jones," Nancy said to the caretaker's back. No reply came from the little man as he shuffled toward the stairs.

"The Creep," Nancy whispered. "Even though he spends his free time in his room over the garage, he really gives me the willies when he appears so suddenly. He actually earns his nickname."

"Well, I suppose he's harmless and he never complains," Heather said, taking a deep breath of the fresh outdoor air. "Oh, don't forget, we're babysitting for the Packers tonight."

"Yeah. They're leaving early," Nancy reminded her, "so we can eat at their cottage instead of the dining room. I feel better already."

They had no idea that they were being observed from the smoking lounge. "What I want to know, is how do Nancy and Heather get off baby-sitting when they are supposed to be campused, too," Jennifer complained. Sheila figured that Jennifer resented their closeness and off-time together, although she could never picture Jennifer babysitting.

"They still don't leave the campus," Sheila said.

"It's been less than one week and I'm climbing the walls," Audrey muttered, pacing around the lounge.

"Come on now," Sheila teased, "where would you go if you could?"

"Anywhere. You wouldn't understand. You don't care about anything just as long as your stomach is full. Have you forgotten about Miss Hicks' gentle sufficiency rule?"

"Those lucky stiffs," Sheila exclaimed, ignoring the barb. "I bet Mrs. Packer will leave all kinds of stuff for them to eat." When the other two girls slammed out of the lounge, Sheila was left wondering what she had said this time.

The girls walked in silence until Nancy noticed a side road. "I never saw that road before," she said, "I wonder where it goes."

"No time like the present to find out," Heather answered cheerfully. "You know, this is one of the few times since you came here that we haven't been loaded up with snow. That's probably why you didn't see it before."

"I'll bet it was used for logging in the old days," Nancy said. On either side of them were towering pines and naked gleaming birches. The edge of the dirt road was still trimmed with snow.

"No logging around here. Probably it led into an old estate owned by the Hicks family that might have burned down or something." The road had become more difficult to follow and the girls strained to see ahead.

"I wonder if we're still actually on school grounds."

"I'm sure we are. Miss Hicks owns hundreds of acres."

"It'd be just my luck to meet Miss Wade coming the other way," Nancy remarked with a grimace. "Remember, I told you about our last talk? Well, even though she is really psycho about religion, I must admit that she seems to draw a lot of strength from it."

"Do you believe in God?"

"Yes, in a way. Actually... What was that?" Startled, Heather stopped and tipped her head to one side.

"What did you hear?" Nancy halted too, her dark eyes alarmed.

"Didn't you hear anything?"

"No. But maybe we ought to go back. We've been gone quite a while. Oh, Lord, now I hear it. There's something in the woods."

"It's probably just an animal. Come on let's start back. I wonder if there are any 'bars in these here parts'."

The girls laughed nervously at Heather's attempt at humor, turned to retrace their steps, and then stopped short.

Five teenage boys, no more than twenty yards away, stood grouped beside the road, staring at them. They were all smoking and laughing uproariously as one of them made a show of rubbing the front of his pants.

Nancy clutched Heather's arm and squeezed it. "What'll we do? What'll we do?" she hissed.

"Don't worry," Heather told her, "they're just a bunch of Townies. I'll take care of them." She raised her voice, speaking with an authority Nancy knew she did *not* feel.

"You boys are on Winthrop Academy property, so you'd better leave before you're caught. And there is no smoking allowed. You're in real trouble."

"You boys better get off our property or someone will punish you," the tallest of the group mocked her.

A dark haired boy stared at Nancy with a sullen, James Dean copycat expression. "What're you babes gonna do to us?" he said.

"Hey, Bobby, I think they're looking for trouble," the boy in the blue sweater announced.

"Yeah, Al, and I've got just the right amount of trouble," a fair-haired boy said as he cupped his crotch.

"That one's mine," Bobby said, pointing at Nancy as he clicked his tongue on the roof of his mouth.

"Heather, what'll we do? Make them go away."

Nancy never took her eyes off the boys.

"Don't be scared," Heather told her. "They wouldn't dare do anything. If we ignore them, they'll just go."

"I want to get away from here. They're going to get us if we don't."

"Please don't panic. This is nothing. Really. Get on the other side of me so I'll be the closest when we walk right by them." Nancy remained frozen in place.

"Hey, girls, why don't you *make* us get off your precious school grounds?" Junior yelled.

"Yeah, you make us, and we'll make you," Al called.

The boys laughed and edged forward.

When Heather spoke again, Nancy heard a tremor in her high-pitched voice. "If you don't get out of here, we're going to report you."

"Oh dear, fellows, they're gonna report us," a boy with curly red hair called.

"I'm scared shitless, Red. How 'bout the rest of you?"

Nancy blocked them from her mind. No names, no faces. They were just stupid Townies. Besides, Heather would save them.

The tallest boy stepped forward. "Maybe they'll beat us up, too."

"My, my, it might hurt." Red laughed

"Time for some action," Bobby said

Taking Nancy's hand, Heather started to pass them.

"Look at that long sexy hair," the one they called Junior said. "Wouldn't you like to run your fingers through that?"

"Like I said, she's mine."

"I go for blondes myself."

"Yeah, look at them tits on that one."

"They're both pretty well stacked."

"We've found ourselves a couple of real cool queens, fellows," Bobby announced with a cigarette bouncing between his lips.

"Oh, I think we can take care of 'em." The tallest of them flicked his cigarette away as he spoke.

Nancy's fear grew when she saw Heather's determination

falter. Yet on some level it got through to her that Heather would get them back to safety.

"If you don't get away from us, we'll scream," Heather shouted now.

No one could hear them. Nancy was sure of that. But perhaps she was trying to frighten the boys.

"Oh, eeeeek, I'm so scared," Red mimicked her voice.

"Yeah, I'm shakin' all over," Junior added.

"You girls bug us 'cause you're so unfriendly."

"Maybe they'd like to dance. How 'bout it, ladies?" Bobby bowed stiffly.

Nancy grabbed hold of Heather's arm. "Go," she whispered. "Go now."

"Okay. We're going to walk right by them," Heather told her, "then we'll run. Ready?"

Nancy thought she could do this as long as they didn't get separated.

As the girls approached, the boys formed a line across the road, arm over shoulder, and began kicking their legs in the air like cancan dancers.

Nancy knew she would remember everything about this moment till the day she died.

"If you won't dance with us, we'll dance for you..."

"Yeah, maybe we could come up and do a show for the school."

"We could do all kinds of shows."

"Sure, we'll show you anything you want to see."

Nancy's eye pleaded with Heather as she watched her friend summon her last bit of courage. "You boys are despicable and loathsome," she said, "and you'd better let us by or you'll be in big trouble."

Now the boys swayed, and rotated their hips back and forth.

"They're going to get us." Nancy's voice verged on hysteria. "It's too late."

"Hey, I wanna dance, whether they want to or not," Bobby shouted, "what d'ya say, guys?"

"Same here. I'm horny as hell."

"How about a waltz."

"Don't forget to share the goods. Don't be piggy."

Bobby flicked his cigarette down and stepped on it. His gaze never left Nancy.

"Okay, I want the one who doesn't have anything to say," Junior cried.

Bobby shoved him aside. "She's mine, I told you."

"Yours, *first*," the tallest added.

"Yeah, just first, Bobby," Al said. "I'm next!"

Nancy wouldn't let go of Heather's arm until Bobby twisted her fingers backward, the pain forcing her to release her grip. Pulling her rigid body against him, Bobby proceeded to dance around in circles.

Two more boys rushed at Heather who tripped and fell, sprawling face first on the dirt road.

They picked her up, one by her hands and the other by her feet and rocked her like a hammock back and forth, higher and higher.

"Up, up and away we go," they chanted.

"Higher, you guys, I can see her pussy."

The other boys clapped in fast rhythm as Bobby twirled Nancy around, her feet above the ground. She was like a mannequin, her body stiff, eyes open but seeing nothing.

"Dance me around again, Tilly..."

Nancy heard Heather crying out for help as she kicked her feet in fury.

"All right, you guys, it's our turn."

"Yeah, I wanna get my hands on them tits."

"You suppose girls with money got bigger boobs?"

"You know it, man. When ya' got money, ya' got bigger and better everything."

Suddenly, with no warning, Nancy turned into a wild creature. She emitted a blood-curdling shriek that began as a guttural sound deep in her throat, and rose steadily to such a crescendo that everything came to a stop.

"Well, well. The little one has come alive."

"Hand her over, Bobby, it's my turn."

Nancy began to struggle at last. She kicked, bit, scratched, and clawed at anything that touched her, fighting with all her might. But, her newfound strength and resistance only seemed to excite them.

Heather sobbed uncontrollably as the boys continued to swing her by her hands and feet. The other three boys, excited by the Nancy's resistance, pulled her to the ground.

"Christ, she's a spit-fire."

"Grab her hair."

"Jesus, her foot almost caught me in the balls."

"Shut her up, that noise is awful."

"Put her down there and I'll shut her up, good."

One of the boys got hold of Nancy's hair, and wrenched her head backward. Her eyes rolled up into her head, her body went limp and they dropped her to the ground. The boys stared down at her motionless form, momentarily stupefied.

"You've killed her," Heather screamed. The boys had lowered her to the ground but she was too dizzy to move.

"Geez, her eyes are open and all you can see is the white."

"We didn't wanna hurt anybody."

"Yeah, we was just havin' a little fun."

"We didn't do nothing to her, really."

"She's breathing, anyway."

"We better get the hell out of here."

Heather dragged herself to her feet. "I'll remember all your faces forever," she sobbed. "Go away."

They backed off as she staggered toward her unconscious friend.

"Come on, you guys, let's lam outta here."

With that, they were gone.

Nancy was screaming as if she had been stung by a hundred yellow jackets.

"Please Nancy. You're in shock. My God, you've got to stop that yelling. I want to get us back to school. Stop it!" Desperate to snap her out of it, Heather shook her friend who suddenly leaped to her feet and bolted down the road, adrenaline coursing through her body.

Uncertain as to why, but thankful that she at last was in motion, Heather raced after her.

"I can't keep up," she heard Heather gasp. "Please Nancy, wait for me. I can't run any further."

Heather walked the last quarter mile. As she rounded the bend that approached the school driveway, she found Nancy waiting quietly by the stone wall.

"Thank God," Heather exclaimed breathlessly. "Are you okay? I didn't know where you'd gone. Come on, we've got to get to the Packers. I think I'd die if we had to sit around in the corridor tonight. Not after what just happened. Those dirty bastards! We can't tell anyone about this. Right?"

Nancy did not reply. Who would she tell? Her mother? Jennifer? What a silly idea. Of course Nancy wouldn't tell anyone. Those horrible boys. Could one of them be the guy Sheila wanted to take to the dance?

"We've got to calm down before we get there, Nancy. Close your eyes and take three deep breaths." Heather leaned toward Nancy, smoothing her hair and picking pine needles off her sweater. "Let's do two more really deep ones and then we'll go."

The Packers didn't seem to notice anything unusual as they gave last minute instructions to the girls. Their meal was in the kitchen, they said, the baby was asleep in her crib, and should sleep through the night. They might be back rather late.

Nancy wondered how could the Packers just blithely hand over their baby to someone like her, someone who couldn't even protect herself, no less an innocent baby.

The two girls sat in the Packer's living room, too stunned by what had happened to move.

"What will I tell mother this time?" Nancy's expressionless voice broke the silence.

"We don't have to tell anybody if we don't want to," Heather told her.

"But she'll know. Eventually, she'll know. And my mother will never believe how it really happened."

"Nancy, what do you mean?"

"What if I'm pregnant again? Nancy said, staring down at her clenched hands.

"My God, Nancy, what are you saying? Do you think that those boys...? Oh you poor thing. Did you think they raped you?"

"They must've. "

"Nancy, you've got to listen to me and believe what I say," Heather insisted. "They didn't rape you. I swear to you that nothing happened."

"But I was lying on my back, like with Philip..."

"No. They pulled your hair so hard your head hit the ground. You were knocked unconscious for a minute."

Nancy reached up to feel the back of her head. "Unconscious?"

Heather rushed on; "That's why they ran away. They were afraid that you were hurt. Honestly, I'd tell you Nancy, only there's nothing to tell. You've got to put that out of your mind 'cause it never happened. Honest Injun. I swear it."

"Oh Heather..."

Nancy's throat ached with relief. She flung herself at Heather, pressing her face against the shelter of her mature breasts. Heather had saved her from a fate worse than death.

Heather's eyes filled with tears as she folded Nancy in her arms. The two girls sobbed together, finding solace in one another.

"Everything is so awful," Nancy wailed against Heather's shoulder.

"I know, I know, Nancy. But we'll be okay."

Nancy breathed deeply. She felt as though her friend could shield her from everything bad. They had just shared a terrifying experience and survived it. Nothing more. She could see that now. "I'm such a jerk," she said softly.

"I was scared, too, you know," Heather told her.

"Maybe I'll never get over what happened. The baby, I mean. "

"You helped me put the pieces of my life back on track. And you can do it for yourself, too. I love you, Nancy."

These words poured over Nancy like a balm. However, she remained within Heather's gentle, protective embrace.

"I love you too, Heather. I'm so afraid of the future. It's like I'm waiting for the final blow. Oh, I can't explain..." Nancy snuggled against Heather and sighed. "There isn't anything wrong with the way we feel about each other, is there, Heather?"

"You're not thinking of lesbians, are you?"

"No, I just wasn't sure," Nancy murmured. "I've never loved anyone like this before. Not my mother. Not Philip. Certainly not Joannie. And I never had a chance with my baby."

"There's nothing to worry about, Nancy," Heather's voice was tender. "We're just two people who are best, best friends." They relaxed against each other.

This day had almost been too much for her, Nancy thought. She felt close to a break down. Drawing away, she smiled with weary contentment.

"Enough of this mutual admiration society," Heather said, grinning. "I'm the greatest and you're the greatest. We just can't help ourselves. Besides, I'm absolutely famished."

The girls fell against one another in a laughing attack, thankful to bring an end to the flood of emotion that had just engulfed them. Without their noticing, night had fallen, and they hadn't even thought to turn on the lights.

Later, while Heather fixed them a snack in the kitchen, Nancy peeked in on the sleeping infant. So sweet. So peaceful. She leaned over the side of the crib and gently stroked the baby's cheek. So tender. So vulnerable... Yes, vulnerable, just like Nancy and Heather had been in the woods. But they had stuck together and made it through the experience. Hopefully Nancy's little baby girl was with someone like Heather, someone who would stand by her always.

CHAPTER EIGHT

Saturday noon meals were quite informal. The girls dressed casually and could leave the table when they finished eating rather than having to wait for Miss Hicks to dismiss them with a nod of her head.

For the past week, Jennifer and Karen were the only girls from the corridor assigned to Jonathan Herrick's table. Jennifer was sure that Karen was unaware of the undercurrent between her and Mr. Herrick. She would be shocked to learn of their intimate relationship, even though she probably saw that Jennifer was an outrageous flirt.

"What a magnificent day," Karen remarked.

"It's about time for some good weather, seeing it's the middle of March," Jennifer said.

"Ooh," Karen said, "don't mention the date. Mid-terms start on Monday and I'm simply not ready."

"To quote Miss Hicks, 'If you're not ready now, all the cramming in the world won't help,'" Jennifer said, with a mischievous glance at Jonathan.

"Truer words were never said," he agreed, glancing around the table to see if anyone noticed Jennifer's too familiar smile. He needed to emphasize to her again the importance of keeping their secret sacrosanct.

"Well, I'm going to take a long walk this afternoon," Jennifer announced, "if I may quote Miss Hicks' very fine advice once again, 'to ventilate the corridors of my mind.'"

"Hey, sounds like a great idea," Karen enthused. "Maybe I'll go with you."

Jennifer hesitated, not wanting to arouse Karen's suspicions. "Okay. What time can you leave?"

Although he seemed disinterested, Jonathan Herrick listened intently to the casual conversation. Both Jonathan and Jennifer were anxious for their meeting that afternoon and he had complete faith that she would be able to shake Karen. It had been his experience that she had the ability to deal with any awkward situation.

"Right after I finish copying my term paper," Karen said. "It shouldn't take more than half an hour once I get started. It's twelve-fifteen now. How about one o'clock?"

"Oh golly, I was planning to leave immediately. I have to be back here at four. Tell you what. I'll go ahead, and we'll probably meet somewhere along the way."

"Right-o. See you later. Excuse me, Mr. Herrick."

Jennifer was, Jonathan thought, an incredibly bright girl, always thinking ahead, never at a loss for an answer. Yet with all her cleverness, she was much more vulnerable than people thought. How beautiful she looked today. Every day, for that matter, he corrected himself.

Excusing herself from the table, Jennifer sauntered out of the dining room. Jonathan watched her exit over the rim of his glass. She was the only girl he knew that really looked good in dungarees. Her waist was tiny and thoughts of her rounded hips started a tingle that he must not allow to show.

My God, he knew he must stop thinking or he'd have to sit there another ten minutes. He directed his attention to the remaining girls and their silly chatter, trying not to let them see that his mind was elsewhere. If only time would pass faster, he could hold Jennifer in his arms again.

Jennifer closed her bedroom door, hoping to insure her privacy. Not that she hadn't taken care of Karen, who had never suggested going on a walk before. Wouldn't you know that she'd choose *this* day to be chummy? And she knew that Nancy, who was always with Heather, wouldn't come barging in. Before, she might have resented her roommate's absence but not any more. Now she'd have to hurry.

In the shower, she wondered if Jonathan was concerned that she wouldn't be able to meet him because of Karen. It amused her that he had pretended not to listen.

It was a wonderful warm feeling to know that at last, someone worthwhile cared about her. She was sure that it was not just sex. It might have started that way. But now he was putting his job on the line for her. He couldn't wait to be with her.

Jennifer hummed while she stepped into the first cotton dress of the season. She knew that she looked radiant. Because of Jonathan, a sense of security that she had never known before had taken root inside her.

She assured herself that they had a future and smiled at the memory of watching Jonathan read a flight manual in study hall yesterday afternoon. It's going to be a glorious summer for a change.

There would be no need to compete for the attention of the most popular boy at the country club. She had been wild, making sure she always got what she wanted. Now, there would be no more of that because she belonged to Jonathan. And that homely, but wonderful honest man would never find another girl who could want him as she did. Not like handsome Doctor Daddy who had women of all ages falling at his feet, leaving Mumsie to find her own fulfillment. With Jonathan, she would never be in that position. Maybe she would learn to fly and they could...She looked at her watch. Uh oh, she'd better scram or Karen would catch her leaving the dorm.

A last glance in the mirror told Jennifer that she was ready. She wanted to look beautiful for Jonathan, not just today, but every day. She slipped an apple green cardigan around her shoulders. She promised herself not to mention love first. Real love. Could it actually be happening to her? She was glad that she hadn't told the girls anything about it.

Jennifer left her room in a daze of anticipation.

One final check having assured Jonathan everything was in order, he decided to take a shower although he had already done so once that morning. He'd better step lively because Jennifer had to leave the dorm before one o'clock in order to avoid Karen. He also decided on a close shave because her skin was so tender and soft. It had been crimson when she had left him last Sunday.

How lucky could any man be, he asked himself as he shaved? He did not, however, question what appeared to be his fate...even if it was beauty and the beast.

As he stepped out of his shower, an unusual calm came over him. He felt confident. Being certain was a new experience. It was not just about him, but also about the relationship...he was sure that Jennifer felt it too. He patted Old Spice on his face.

It was amazing how much Jennifer had changed, he thought. She was no longer sharp or cynical. In the classroom and at the dining table, she was happier, mellower. The only answer was that her feelings for him had brought about the change. *She was in love with him.* But he must not rush her. If he became too insistent about what she meant to him, he might frighten her away. Besides, he had to keep this relationship clandestine. No one must even suspect. He must be careful to protect both of them. And his job.

Jonathan Herrick roused himself from his thoughts, chagrined that his groin was pulsating. He determined not to rush into anything. This wasn't just about sex, he assured himself; she had an amazingly alert, inquisitive mind, as well as beauty. He laughed aloud, thinking that he no longer needed Scotch for courage.

He chose two of his favorite records and set them on the turntable of his hi-fi. He had just turned Jimmie Rodgers down low in readiness for Jennifer's arrival when she slipped in through the kitchen door. Thank God she was here and his life could begin again.

She leaned against the door, placing her hand under her left breast. "Oh, my heart is beating so fast."

"I'm awfully glad it is," he teased.

"No. I mean it's pounding. Just as I was going down the back stairs of the dorm, I heard Karen's voice in the corridor. So I ran all the way down here and, of course, I had to cut around through the woods."

"You poor dear. Come here." He reached for her.

Wrapping her arms around his waist, she rested her head against his chest.

"Your heart is pounding, too," she whispered, and stood on tiptoe to kiss him on the cheek.

"Hello."

"Hi there. So glad you were able to accept my invitation."

"Believe me, we almost had company."

"Come on." He took her hand and led her into the living room.

They sat in the middle of the long couch and faced one another. Jennifer curled her legs demurely under her skirt. "It's such a gorgeous day," she said, "I wish we didn't have to hide away. It would be fun just to go for a walk."

"There's nothing I'd like better. But we both know how important it is to guard our secret. It's absolutely imperative. You do understand, don't you, Jen?"

"Of course," Jennifer assured him.

"You look charming today as usual," he said, studying her long glossy nails. "What are your plans for the April vacation? It's right around the corner now."

"Oh I don't know," she shrugged, "I have several choices. I'm in no hurry to decide. Why? What are you going to do?"

"I'm in no hurry to decide either," Jonathan told her.

"Want anything to drink?" he asked.

"No thanks, I feel intoxicated enough."

"That isn't the kind of drink I meant and you know it," he said returning to his spot next to her.

"I know," she told him, laughing. "The music is divine. Let's dance."

Jumping to her feet, Jennifer took both his hands in hers in an attempt to pull him up.

"No. Wait. I need to close the drapes," he said. "Someone might see us."

Jennifer's smile vanished. He sounded so curt, almost as though he was accusing her of being indiscrete. In a moment, all the warm intimacy had vanished. She was silent.

"Jennifer dearest, please forgive me," he said apologetically. "It's hard to explain how much my position here means to me. I didn't come from a background like yours. I worked my way through college and fought my way up the academic ladder. I just cannot be careless now." He knelt in front of the couch, his eyes bore deep into hers. "Forgive me? Please?"

"Jonathan, it is you who should forgive me," she said, taking his face in her hands. "I take too much for granted. Please be patient with me."

"Okay, so let's just close the stupid drapes!"

In the golden semi-darkness, Jennifer and Jonathan danced. She stood on tiptoe while he stooped to meet her. Their bodies swayed, while the plaintive voice of Pat Boone enveloped them with *April Love*.

They came to a stop as he began to kiss her.

"Have you truly forgiven me, Jennifer dearest?" he breathed in her ear.

"Oh yes," she told him. "I do understand. I promise I will never do anything to hurt you, Jonathan, or jeopardize your job."

With a fresh rush of ardor, he gently caressed her hair, her cheek, her neck. She quivered as he awakened every nerve under her skin. He reached around to cup the curve of her buttocks in his hands.

"The first thing I noticed about you was your behind," he told her. "I wanted to touch you more than you can imagine." He was fully aroused now. It took so little when he was with her.

"Jonathan," Jennifer murmured. "Let's get undressed. We can dance like this, naked with nothing between us."

"Yes, yes." He was frantic to remove his clothes, at the same time unable to take his eyes from Jennifer as she tossed her dress aside and stepped out of her pink silk and lace panties.

"You are glorious," he moaned. His eyes devoured her. "I want to memorize every curve and crevice of your body."

Suddenly feeling self-conscious, Jennifer embraced him, and hid herself against his lanky form. Her body was soft and pliant against his and she pressed her lips against his shoulder as they moved as one.

No longer dancing, Jonathan bent forward to tighten his arms around her. He ran his tongue over her lips while his fingers caressed her face. She opened her mouth. The taste of her was sweet and warm as her tongue flicked to meet his; her breath light and fast, his was ragged with excitement. Unable to restrain himself any longer, Jonathan carried her into the bedroom.

"Take hold of me, darling."

Her cool fingers closed around him, she tugged gently, and then pushed back.

He ran his hand up her slim white thigh, then down her leg. Her muscles were rigid and covered with a patina of perspiration. He put his hands under her hips, pressing himself inside her. His stomach muscles tightened as she raised her body to meet his. They sighed together. The gratification was beyond anything either had ever experienced.

They did not speak as their bodies relaxed.

Jennifer sighed. "That was beautiful, Jonathan." She turned on her side to look at his face.

"It was because of you, dearest."

They lay silent for a moment, reveling in the closeness of body and spirit.

"Hey, I have the most fantastic idea." Jennifer exclaimed suddenly. "What do you think of us meeting somewhere during spring vacation? We can be very discreet about it and it can be anywhere you say. Anywhere."

"Well, maybe that could work." Jonathan told her. "How do you know your parents would let you go wherever you choose?"

Jennifer shrugged. "That's the least of our problems," she said. "My loving parents are so delighted when I take them up on their trip offers, that it's irrelevant what the destination is. You know, anything to be rid of the burden of 'entertaining' their daughter at home for ten days. After all, they are terribly busy."

"Are you always that bitter when it comes to your parents?" he asked.

"I suppose," Jennifer said. "But I don't give a damn about them anymore. Oh Jonathan, it would be such fun. Where shall we go?"

"How about Bermuda?"

"Too much risk of running into some of the other girls. My parents aren't the only ones who are at a loss as to what to do with a teenage kid for a few days."

Jennifer hesitated for a moment, wondering if cost would be a problem for Jonathan. She guessed that private school salaries weren't that much. Certainly she didn't want to be a financial burden to him.

"In the past, my parents have actually paid another girl's way just to be company for me," she told him. "I could ask for two tickets. They'd be in the next mail, I'm certain of it."

He frowned. "No. I'm not taking charity from your parents or anyone else."

"I didn't mean it to sound like that," Jennifer protested. "They'd never know the difference. I thought it would be a good joke on them if *they* actually financed my "tramp behavior." She broke off, as though uncertain of his response.

"Well it's no joke," Jonathan told her stiffly. "I'm capable of paying my own way. Why do you think my position here is so important? It gives me financial freedom to do whatever I want to do. Something I never knew before. And once we get wherever it is that we are going," he added, "you'll be my guest. I feel strongly about this, Jennifer, so please don't argue."

"I'm not," she protested.

"All right. Now, I have an idea. It's something I've wanted to do for a long time. Let's get dressed and I'll tell you about it." Jonathan began to get up but Jennifer pulled him back to the bed. She leaned her elbows on either side of his head; her tumbled hair fell forward, brushing his face.

"This is the most wonderful thing that has ever happened to me Jonathan. I just want you to know."

"It is for me, too," he told her. "During all those years of trying to establish myself, I never dared to hope for a relationship. I have so little to offer."

"How can you say that?"

"Well, it happens to be the truth," he said, grinning. "Now, do you want to hear my idea or not?"

"Tell me now, or am I too heavy, lying on top of you?"

Jonathan laughed. "You're like a feather. But I think we'd better get dressed. I *do* have company once in a while, you know."

"We could always say that you are tutoring me for exams."

"As if you needed help. You know, I really admire your creativity and brains."

He laughed as she bounded off him and entered the bathroom.

"Now tell me your marvelous idea," she said, a few minutes later, sitting down on the couch beside him, prim and graceful.

"Well, I've wanted to go to Mexico ever since I read about an "undiscovered" fishing village on the west coast called Mazatlan. The Air Force whetted my appetite for travel, but obviously I haven't done much up till now."

"It sounds terrific," she said, bouncing with childish excitement. "Let's do it."

"We'd have to meet there instead of traveling together, naturally."

"Naturally," she mocked. "We must be circumspect. Careful, or you'll sound like Miss Hicks."

"I'll just ignore that comment. Anyway, we'd have to fly to Mexico City, stay overnight, and then fly to Mazatlan the next morning."

"I can't wait till vacation. I'll call my parents tonight and the ticket will be in the mail by Monday. I guess I'll say I'm staying in Mexico City and then I'll catch a flight to Mazatlan on my own. Where will we stay?"

"There is one luxury hotel called La Playa, right on the beach," Jonathan said happily. He couldn't believe this was really happening.

"I'll find it, darling. I can hardly wait."

"Me too."

Their kiss was warm and full of promise.

"I'd better bomb out of here right now," Jennifer said. "Where does the time go when we're together?"

"I hate to tell you this," Jonathan said following her into the kitchen, "but I got roped into conducting a review class tomorrow afternoon so we won't be able to meet again until next weekend." Jennifer's smile faded. They had so much to talk about and never enough opportunity. Being in Mexico together for the whole vacation was her idea of heaven.

"Of course," she said, regaining her composure. "I understand. I don't have to like it but after all, you are a teacher here. Besides, it wouldn't hurt me to put a little time into my studies, particularly since exams begin on Monday."

She tried to sound adult, knowing that he expected it of her, but it was difficult to hide her intense disappointment.

At the back door, he gathered her in his arms again. "Darling," he said, "each time we are together, it is harder for me to be restrained in public. But what we have must be protected. No matter what, we must not give our secret away."

"It means the world to me, too. Just think, only three more weeks and then...paradise. See you at dinner tonight."

With that, she was gone, leaving the door open behind her, meager proof that she had been there at all.

"I'm going to marry her!" he exclaimed aloud as though he had made a brilliant discovery. "I am going to marry Jennifer." His voice rose this time with the confidence and pride of a man who had made a decision he meant to keep.

CHAPTER NINE

Nancy looked around the smoking lounge in disbelief. "They can't do that to us, can they?" she said.

"They not only can, but they do," Sheila insisted, taking three brownies out of the box her mother sent before passing it to the other girls. She was thankful Sam had forgotten to check her laundry box this week.

"Do what?" Karen asked as she entered the lounge and flopped onto the nearest chair.

"They were telling me that if you get caught studying for a test after lights out, you'll be docked twenty percent of the mark that you get in that particular subject?"

"It sure is true," Karen replied. "Isn't it awful?"

"Awful? I think it's outrageous. I've never heard of anything so unfair. College won't be like that next year. At least Miss Hicks should cancel regular classes during exam week so we could put in extra study time." Nancy slumped in her chair, twirling a strand of her long hair over a well-chewed pencil.

"That's a great suggestion, but they have turned that idea down for years now," Audrey said, lighting another cigarette with the tip of the last one.

"If mid-terms are like this," Nancy groaned, "I can imagine what finals are like." The girls sat in dejected acceptance.

Heather picked up her history book, staring at it with distaste. "All the cramming in the world couldn't help me memorize this stuff. It seems like such a waste of time."

"I like American History," Nancy said, "but I'm certainly with Heather that it's stupid to make us memorize so many details."

Everyone grumbled in agreement as they consumed the remains of Sheila's brownies. Audrey looked over two before choosing the one with the most walnuts showing.

"I'm going to take this box to the barrel out back and get rid of the evidence," Sheila said. She tapped the crumbs to one corner and was shaking them into her mouth as the door closed behind her.

"In the words of our beloved headmistress," Jennifer told them, "we may not be aware of the significance or value of what Winthrop Academy offers while we are young, but if we are not wise enough to take advantage of our education before we are thrust into the cruel, unsympathetic, demanding world, we will find ourselves failing in college and unable to meet the mandates of society." She was wagging her finger as she spoke. "We must fortify ourselves now for the trials ahead by recognizing...'"

"For Christ sakes Jennifer, take a break," Audrey interrupted, "you sound just like her. One Miss Hicks is about all I can handle." She stood up and shook out each leg as though getting ready for a race.

Sheila barged back into the smoking lounge. "Phew! It sure stinks in here...who farted?" Her arms were full of books which she dropped on the floor, laughing loud guffaws as though she was listening to comedy hour. She plopped onto the couch, pulled out her Camels, and reached across Heather for the Zippo lighter resting on the table.

"She who smelt it, dealt it, Fatso," Audrey replied and faster than a speeding bullet, she snatched the lighter from the table.

"Christ, I was just being funny. You don't have to be a bitch about it. Gimmie that thing." Sheila made a half-hearted lunge toward Audrey and then she slumped back.

"Come on you guys, cut it out." Nancy handed Sheila her lighter. "Everyone is getting uptight over exams."

"I still say that after we leave here...whether we end up as teachers, nurses, or housewives...it makes no difference if we know that the Molasses Act was in 1733 or 1763," Heather argued.

"Yeah," Sheila agreed. "Who gives a damn about the

Molasses Act anyway? She got out her study notes. "By the way, which date is correct?" Her pen was poised.

"I don't know and could care less," Heather told her. "We just spend too much time remembering *when* it happened instead of concerning ourselves with *why* it happened. Let's face it, I just hate history." Nancy was surprised by this exposition since Heather usually kept her opinions to herself. Their friendship had helped both girls come out of themselves, to be more open and natural than before.

"It was 1733," Jennifer said in an off-handed manner.

Karen closed her eyes and yawned. "We may as well accept the fact that we were sent here to obtain a classical education."

"Maybe for you, but that certainly doesn't pertain to the rest of us. So what's been thrown at us in the name of education is definitely nothing we'd choose to know."

Once again, Audrey thought bitterly of her parents whose divorce and separate careers were the cause of her being at Winthrop Academy. But maybe that was only one of the reasons.

"Boy, I can just see Karen at the P.T.A. meetings or the Young Adults Educational Seminars priding herself at knowing the date when Isaac Newton was bopped on the head with the apple," Jennifer said, laughing. I mean, this is really putting the classical education to fine use."

She grabbed Karen's history book, placed it on top of her head and shuffled around the room with arms extended from her sides for balance.

"You guys can make all the wisecracks you want," Karen said, taking the book off Jennifer's head, "but I think it's a matter of your attitude toward learning. Regardless of why you're here, you should take advantage of what they offer. I know I sound corny, but I agree with Miss Hicks."

"I was just joking, Karen," Jennifer admitted. "Well, instead of all this talk, I'll try a little study action. Au revoir, mes petites."

Nancy was amazed how her roommate had backed down. She had changed so much lately. No more talk about attracting

Mr. Herrick, or as a matter of fact, anything to do with sex. Jennifer had been nice, yet rather distant. She's probably spending a lot of time in the library, boning up for exams.

Sheila gave a long loud whistle. "Well, in all my born days, I never thought I'd hear Jennifer Stewart apologize to anyone. Now I've seen everything." She glanced at her watch. "Oh, my gosh, Audrey, we're supposed to be in Herrick's review class, right now."

Watching the two girls rush frantically out the door together, it occurred to Nancy that they actually liked one another.

"Well folks," Heather said, hugging her history book to her chest, "there's no time like the present."

"Off to the dungeon," Nancy added, as she followed her out of the lounge. Standing in the hallway, Nancy stopped to look out the window. "What a beautiful day, Heather. It's too nice to be inside. Phew, what's that smell? Oh no!"

The two girls saw Mr. Jones poking along with three empty wastebaskets, head bent as usual. Nancy's hand flew to her mouth in embarrassment.

"Hello, Mr. Jones," she said. "Come on Heather, we've got to get going on our studies." They scurried off to Heather's room and flopped onto her bed. Nancy picked up Heather's stuffed kitten and hugged it.

"Heavens, I hope he didn't hear me," Nancy said, trying to balance the kitten on her knee. "There's something frightening about The Creep."

"You know we always exaggerate about him," Heather replied absently. "He's harmless."

How could she know that, Nancy asked herself? She had been wrong about the intentions of those boys from town, hadn't she? *They* weren't harmless.

"He wouldn't be here if he wasn't," Heather insisted.

"Oh, you're probably right," Nancy conceded, "but you must admit it's odd not to talk...ever. His weirdness is hard to put your finger on, but it's there. Any way, let's not talk about him. Heather, remember what Sheila said about Jennifer in the lounge? Well, I think it's true. Haven't you noticed a change in her?"

"Now that you mention it, yes. She doesn't swear as much or seem so bitter. Maybe, to quote Miss Hicks, she has reached that 'glorious age of reason and maturity.'"

Looking at her friend, Nancy saw the person she would like to be. She had so much to give with her spontaneous warmth and understanding. It was like an electric current that flowed through her. Because of Heather, her feelings of self assurance were improving. Daily.

"I wish I was your sister," she said.

Heather' eyes lit up. "Me too. Things are so much better between my dad and me, especially now that I have you. That's what it was, you know. Pure jealousy. I'm ashamed when I think of how I acted with Eleanor."

"What about their baby?" Nancy asked. Her face was vulnerable, full of memories.

"Of all people, you know best how I acted when I heard about the baby. But I feel differently toward Eleanor now, thanks to you. It's funny, but secretly I'm looking forward to the little thing."

"I must be looking forward to its arrival more than anyone," Nancy said quietly.

Heather rushed across the room to give her friend a reassuring hug. "Nancy," she said, "I have a confession to make. I only pray that you won't be angry with me or misunderstand my motives."

With one arm resting lightly across Nancy's slim shoulder, Heather studied her friend's face intently.

"When I wrote Daddy and Eleanor asking if you could come home with me for spring vacation, I told them all about you."

"How could you?" Nancy said, pulling away. She felt so exposed in the face of what she considered to be the ultimate betrayal.

"Please let me finish," Heather said. "I can't stand to have you look at me that way. Eleanor wrote back to say that if she were your mother, she never would have allowed the baby to leave the family regardless of your decision to marry or not. She said that it's cruel to make someone feel shame over something as beautiful as having a child."

Nancy listened carefully. Her stomach began to tighten and she felt regret swell within her like a fetus. Those feelings would always be there, she knew; the pain of an unwed mother with a child lost to her forever, the bitterness of a mother's contempt.

"The thing is," Heather continued, "they not only want you to come for spring vacation, but they suggested that you spend the summer with us. Oh Nancy, just think how fabulous it would be."

"The whole summer?" Nancy asked. She didn't recognize her own voice. It sounded small and far away.

"Yes. Won't it be fantastic?" Heather took her desk calendar and began to count the days until vacation.

"They really want me, knowing what I did? Nancy asked, incredulous. "Aren't they afraid I'll be a bad influence on you?"

"Now I know you're trying to be funny," Heather said as she reached into her desk for the letter. She ran her finger over the words and stopped half way down the page. "Here's what my father said: 'There, but for the grace of God goes anyone's daughter...' She placed the letter on Nancy's lap.

Nancy's knuckles were white as she gripped it. Her humiliation clung to her like a second skin. "Do you think Eleanor would let me help with the baby?" she asked in a low voice.

"Of course," Heather said, "she mentioned it herself in the letter. After all, she's not getting any younger and she could probably use the help."

Nancy hugged Heather, tears flooding her eyes. "What a beautiful summer it will be. If you're certain they want me."

Just then, Sheila burst into the room and in her usual blundering manner went straight to the point; "How come your name wasn't matched up with a date for the dance, Nancy?" she demanded. "The list came back, you weren't on it. Miss Hicks will black mark you on your citizenship report if you don't go. Besides, you idiot, it could be fun."

"You can't imagine how much I don't want to," Nancy said, looking at her friend for sympathy and support although she guessed that if Heather could have said it in front of Sheila, she would have said that not all boys were like those Townies they had met on the road.

"Hey, some boys are goons and some are really fun, but in either case, these dances are good for a lot of laughs. We all want you to go." It was Heather speaking.

Nancy was not prepared to do anything on Sheila's recommendation, but Heather always seemed to know what was right. Nancy loved the way she had given herself completely to their friendship. The bond between them was, she knew, rare.

"All right," Nancy said. "I'll go."

"Great." Heather and Sheila said simultaneously. "Let's go down right now and speak to the dance chairman."

"Okay," Nancy told them, "but we'd better go now before I change my mind." Nancy couldn't believe what she had just agreed to do. She dreaded the thought of arbitrarily being assigned to spend an evening with a boy, having to make conversation, to let him put his arm around her. Touch her. It wasn't anything she wanted to do. She was going because Heather asked her to. That was the *only* reason.

❧

Exam week was hell. Everyone crammed after lights out. Nancy sneaked into Heather's room with a flashlight. They covered every crevice where light could possibly show, and studied under the covers. Of course, they always listened for Waddles, who patrolled the hall more than usual now. The rule saying that twenty percent would be deducted off the final grade of anyone who was caught studying after hours was incredibly unfair. The girls had to be ingenious to avoid Miss Wade's constant surveillance in the hallway.

As mid-terms got closer, faces grew haggard. The Corridor

Girls had very little to say to one another and their eyes were red-rimmed. No one spent extra time in the smoking lounge. They crawled into bed only when they succumbed to exhaustion.

April drenched the countryside with a driving rain that made the first day of exams even more dismal. The furious downpour soaked the earth forming deep muddy puddles. By early morning, when alarm clocks resounded intermittently throughout the building, the storm had nearly worn itself out. Daylight brought a constant drizzle as the soft rain fell on the still cold earth.

Nancy had fumbled to hit the alarm button in deference to her sleeping roommate. Padding quietly to her desk, she picked up Heather's letter from Eleanor and, holding it to her heart, she leaned against the window. A brown leaf clinging to the far branch of a beech tree captured her attention. It seemed odd and lonely in its proximity to the new, tender buds. She watched as it released its precarious hold, landing next to a clump of yellow crocuses that, just days ago, had risen to greet the spring. Now it was plastered against the rain-soaked earth.

Nancy sighed deeply. I am no longer dead inside. There is something to look forward to now.

Tiptoeing to the closet, Nancy reached into the far corner of the shelf and took out her Bible. Wiping the dust from it, she opened it carefully and tenderly placed Eleanor Brock's letter safely inside.

"I hate to disillusion you, but praying won't help," Jennifer mumbled after watching Nancy curiously for several sleepy minutes.

"Oh I know," Nancy said, flushing, "but at this point, I hardly think cramming will help either."

"The best thing to do is read your notes over once in the morning to refresh your mind and then leave the rest to luck."

Jennifer grinned at her roommate. Nancy really was a nice girl, a little deep, but nice. After vacation, she would make more of an effort to be friendly. Speaking of that, there were less than two more weeks to go. Exams. The dance. And then freedom! She couldn't wait.

"What are you doing for spring break?" Nancy asked as though she had read her mind.

"Probably a trip," Jennifer answered vaguely. "I never know where till the last minute. Where are you going?"

"Heather and her parents have invited me to their home for the week," Nancy announced proudly. "And the summer, too."

"That's great. Sounds like you enjoy going home about as much as I do."

"Well, it's different."

Hearing a slight scratching noise on their door, the girls dove back into their own beds, thinking it might be Miss Wade. Instead, Sheila slipped into the room and closed the door with exaggerated care.

"Do you kids have anything to eat?" she asked. "I've been up studying for hours and I'm absolutely weak from lack of sustenance." She looked hopefully from face to face.

"All I've got is some Tums," Nancy said.

"Well, at least it's something." Sheila accepted the Tums, and popped two in her mouth. "I'm so jittery. Maybe they'll help settle my roaring stomach."

After breakfast, The Corridor was quiet. The only sound was the rustle of papers and muffled groans. At last, Miss Wade left her room and the sound of her heavy steps echoed down the corridor. That ended the final frenzy of cramming. The girls slammed their books closed with resigned sighs. It was time to go.

"The jig is up, ladies; it's now or never," Sheila called out, rounding up her corridor cohorts. "Fill your fountain pens and let's go. It's sink or swim time."

"I'm so tired that I'll probably sleep through my whole first damn exam," Audrey said, staggering into the hall. "I didn't turn out my flashlight till after three this morning."

Heather joined the group. “I’m so nervous. It’s all those dates that get me down.”

“I’ve had diarrhea all morning,” Karen moaned, rubbing her stomach. “What’ll I do if it strikes during the exam? They’ll think I’m going to the john to look at notes or something. Oh, it’s awful.”

“Maybe Miss Wade will go along as a chaperone,” Jennifer teased.

“That’s not even funny,” Nancy said, trying not to laugh.

The Corridor girls started down the hall. They walked close together as though last minute strength and knowledge rested in their unity.

“Oh my God,” Sheila shouted, “I forgot my panda. I‘ll never pass without it. Wait for me...”

❧

The week dragged on marked by dreary weather and increasingly irritable temperaments.

Why these kids think we get some kind of diabolical delight in giving exams, I’ll never know, Jonathan Herrick thought. The faculty is equally as miserable and under as much strain. Most of these girls are totally unaware.

Wearily, he stacked the blue books on his desk, and then he slid his fingers beneath his glasses and massaged his eyes. He stood, stretched, and glanced at his watch. It had been a long day and he was conducting a review class that evening. He decided to go to the cottage and relax before the next onslaught of questions and answers. He turned off the light in his classroom and stepped into the hall.

Holding his briefcase between his feet, he struggled into his jacket. He heard silly giggles from the next classroom.

“Boy, when I get this tired, I always get the simples.”

“Well you better cut it out or we’ll never get through reviewing this damn English and you know how tough Herrick’s exams are.”

“You’re not telling me anything new.”

"You kids better shut up or he'll hear you."

Jonathan smiled. Apparently he had a reputation for being a taskmaster. The voices continued while he quietly paused by the room.

"Herrick's review class was over more than an hour ago," he heard one of the girls say. "He's probably having a rendezvous in some cozy little spot with Jennifer Stewart right now."

"Yeah, English is one exam she won't have to study for."

Suddenly Jonathan felt as though he couldn't breathe. The girls' words bit like acid as the full impact of what he had just heard stunned him. He remained where he was, willing himself to be calm, praying that he had misunderstood.

"She must be pretty hard up to go after a guy like Herrick."

"Yeah, she's so sharp looking; I can't imagine what she sees in him."

"They say opposites attract."

The memory of Jennifer came rushing up from its hiding place and splintered his heart in two. He forced himself to walk passed the door, his lanky frame crashing through the shaft of light as if it were a pane of glass. He tried to comprehend the fact that his affair with Jennifer was common knowledge. That she had obviously told her friends. That she had lied to him. That the world of Winthrop Academy was laughing at him. His long sturdy legs seemed to buckle.

He could feel the blood vessels in his temples pulsating. He had been so convinced that she understood. It was incredible how wrong he had been about trusting her. About believing her. About loving her.

He could not let this happen to him. He had to quash the very idea that he could be involved with Jennifer, or any student for that matter.

CHAPTER TEN

Jonathan Herrick knocked on Miss Hicks' office door. His glasses had slid down the bridge of his nose and he was breathing heavily. When she finally opened the door, his mouth sagged and words failed him.

"What is it, Jonathan?" Miss Hicks asked with alarm, her voice fixed in a tone of dark expectation. "Do come in and sit down. Tell me what's wrong." She nervously smoothed her short hair behind her ears.

Jonathan could only think of one thing. He had to keep his job and preserve his image at any cost. Jennifer had thrown away what they had together. He must concentrate on saving himself. Captain Herrick. In charge.

"Jennifer Stewart cheated," he said flatly.

The lie shocked him. It was as though someone else had said the words. Miss Hicks flopped back heavily in her desk chair. His words struck her like a fist out of the darkness.

"I knew it was bad news," she said. "You're white as a sheet. But Jennifer Stewart? She's received top marks in every subject from her first day here. Why? How did she cheat? Tell me, Jonathan."

"I saw her leaving my classroom just as I was coming down the hall," he said. "The exam I had prepared for her class tomorrow was sitting in a folder on top of my desk." He stopped speaking. His lower jaw quivered.

"Then what?" Miss Hicks urged. A twinge of pain that signaled the onset of a migraine stirred low at the back of her neck.

"She was obviously copying the questions," Jonathan went

on with so much conviction in his voice that he really believed himself.

"Good Heavens," Miss Hicks exclaimed, "I don't think we've ever had an incident of cheating in all my years at Winthrop. What was that child thinking of? She doesn't need to cheat; she's an "A" student."

"Exactly. I was shocked."

"So, what did you do?"

"I came to you immediately, of course."

"You're absolutely right to report such actions," she assured him. "You had no choice. I would expect no less of someone as loyal as you are to this institution."

Miss Hicks walked over to the front window where she stared into the darkness. Why do girls like Jennifer feel obligated to defy authority? She is a senior, so near to graduation. She knows that when anyone breaks a rule, there will be punishment. And it is meted out according to the offense.

Jonathan had done something heinous to protect himself, and now it was out of his hands. No second thoughts allowed. He couldn't let himself crack now.

Miss Hicks pressed her hand hard on the top of her head, as if to ward off the agonizing pain that was on its way. "Well," she said, "there is no alternative. She will have to be expelled. What a pity. Such a waste of precious potential."

Exhausted, she reached for the telephone on her desk. "I'll gather as many faculty members as possible and then I'll call Jennifer," she said. "You will have to make a formal accusation."

Jonathan felt a ripple of sheer terror. Once she was aware of what he had said, the charges he had made, Jennifer might well reveal the truth about their relationship. And when she did, his career would be doomed. He had gained nothing by accusing her as he had done. And he may have lost everything.

A small group of teachers sat in charged silence. They had been summoned late in the evening and the point of why they had been called together hovered perilously around them. Without delay or emotion, Miss Hicks informed them of the circumstances of the meeting.

"The rules are clear," she said, "and so is the offense. I hope that we can have this unfortunate situation dealt with by lights out. I will contact her parents tonight. The sooner she is gone from campus, the sooner this will be behind us."

When the knock came on the door, Miss Hicks hesitated for a moment before opening it.

Jennifer knew at once that something was very wrong. When she said good evening, no one responded. There was a dreadful silence, and at last, Miss Hicks spoke.

"I am afraid, Jennifer," Miss Hicks began, "that we have a distressing report of flagrant disrespect on your part for the basic trust and privileges that we have extended to you as a student at Winthrop Academy. I am painfully disappointed in you Jennifer. We all are."

Jennifer guessed immediately what had happened. Her mind raced frantically. How had she and Jonathan been found out? She resolved that she would protect Jonathan and his job at all costs, even if she had to lie.

"I'm sorry, what did you say?" Jennifer asked the headmistress who had continued to drone on about Winthrop Academy this and Winthrop Academy that.

"Mr. Herrick, will you please relate exactly what happened?" Miss Hicks said, positioning herself so Sam was in full view, needing her approval more than ever.

Jennifer's innocent calm was worse than a protest. Jonathan cleared his throat, floundering in the depths of her silence. When he finally spoke, he chose his words carefully. "Most regretfully, I must report that Miss Stewart has betrayed the rules against cheating at this school."

Through a mist of disbelief, she stared at him in confusion.

Jonathan paused but she didn't speak, so he hurried on. Words came automatically now, without thought, as the last gasp of self-respect spent itself in his haste to be finished.

"Apparently this means immediate dismissal," he told her. "You're such a good student, I'm sorry but it was my duty to report you. Maybe you didn't mean to...I'm so sorry."

Jonathan raised his eyes to meet Jennifer's and saw her staring at him with an expression of complete astonishment. He bore the searching scrutiny with despair. Why didn't she protest, say it's a lie, scream at him, cry, do anything?

Dearest Jennifer, what have I done to us?

A thread of regret needled into his heart. He could never have predicted that he would feel such guilt and remorse. He had not bargained for her self-restraint. That in itself would have destroyed his outrage. He wanted to cover his face with his hands, take back the lies, cancel what he had done. But if he admitted that he had lied, he would be fired. They would suspect the rumors about him and Jennifer were true, and she was not quite eighteen, not even of legal age for a man such as he. *God, what now*? He clenched his teeth, for he suddenly wanted to weep.

Miss Hicks' voice broke as she shattered the silence. "Why, Jennifer? You're an honor student. How could you do this?" She articulated each word carefully, the other staff members murmuring agreement. If only a right answer could obliterate the offense. Her headache was pounding against the back of her eyes.

"Mr. Herrick told you this?"

It was not a question, it was an accusation. Jennifer stared dumbly at Miss Hicks as though they were the only people in the room.

"Of course." Miss Hicks was strangely annoyed. She must be done with this. The strain unnerved her. She wanted to be alone with Sam and sob in her arms. Instead, she straightened her back and reminded herself of Grandmother Elizabeth Hicks' creed as the first headmistress of Winthrop Academy: *Grace Under Pressure.*

The old Jennifer would have struck out, countered one attack with another, put them all, including Jonathan, on the defense. But she couldn't do it. If he had done this thing, made up this lie, he must have done so because he had to. She realized now that no one had convictions so strong that they could not be corrupted.

Oh Jonathan. She glanced at him, and saw him suddenly for what he was, pathetic and manipulative. If his job meant so much to him, then let him have it. She would never care about anyone or anything again.

She held her body rigid. Her mind throbbed with remembrances of their love making. And their plans. How could she have allowed her dreams to take such a powerful hold on her?

Miss Hicks told Jennifer that she was officially expelled, and that she would arrange with her parents for her to be picked up in the morning. And when Jennifer looked directly at Jonathan, he simply stared at her sadly.

Jennifer made herself impervious to Miss Hicks' lecture. It all meant nothing, she told herself. Nothing would change. Life would go on, and Jonathan would fade. He used her. He did not love her.

"After taking your past record into consideration," Miss Hicks told her, "we have decided to allow you to continue your studies at home. Of course you cannot participate in the sacred ritual of our graduation program, but we will send you your diploma."

Miss Hicks hoped Jennifer appreciated this concession. Miss Wade had voted against it, but Sam had told her she thought something was strange about the whole situation with Mr. Herrick's accusation. Sam had insisted that Jennifer should at least be allowed to graduate. She had advised her not to ruin the girl's future. When Sam felt really strongly about something, Miss Hicks didn't argue.

"We will want to be in touch with you," Miss Hicks concluded. "Where were you planning to spend your spring vacation?"

Jennifer, laboring up some deep unprecedented mental slope, was shocked back into reality by Miss Hicks' question. At first, she could not speak. She hesitated as she watched Jonathan, whose eyes riveted on the door in his desperate desire to escape. With careful lack of expression, she managed to answer.

"I'll be in Mexico." Jennifer said with what was for Jonathan, an ominous calm. "As a matter of fact, I think I'll be there indefinitely, all things considered," she added, turning once again to look at Jonathan. Her eyes were so full of contempt that he flinched.

"In that case," Miss Hicks interceded wearily, "we will be in touch with you through your parents until you return from Mexico. I will call them tonight while you pack. They will have to pick you up first thing in the morning. I am sorry Jennifer. We all are." Her voice was neutral, a tone she had perfected. "The only possible good that could come out of your unfortunate mistake is if you have learned a lesson of self-discipline, self-control, and honesty. You may go now." She held up her fingers to dismiss the girl.

Jonathan felt the full impact of what he had done now. Jennifer had not tried to defend herself against his lies. She had not denied them or tried to defame him in any way.

Oh my darling Jennifer, I was so wrong. Please forgive me.

Jennifer's expression remained frozen on her face as though she were unaware of what had happened to her. She politely said good night, left the room, and closed the door behind her without a sound. But after that, she came alive, careening down the empty hall. The events of the past hour were nothing but a blur. She only knew that her heart ached as the image of Jonathan's face slammed into her.

In the solace of her room, she screamed against her pillow.

Long before the wake up bell, Jennifer slid out of bed. Careful not to awaken Nancy who still knew nothing of what had happened to her, Jennifer dressed quietly and left the room, flashlight in hand. Barefooted, she walked boldly through the corridor past Miss Hicks' quarters, down the winding staircase, through the reception hall to Mr. Herrick's classroom. Knowing that he would be there early to correct exams, Jennifer waited.

At five-forty five, Jonathan Herrick pushed open the door. His shoulders were slumped, and he smelled strongly of some kind of liquor. When he saw Jennifer he froze, hugging a pile of bluebooks tightly against his chest.

"Why?" she began plaintively. "How could you have done this to us? Or maybe there never was any "us". Maybe all it ever was to you was sex. And I thought we were in love. Real love."

"Jennifer, dearest," he said, dropping the books on the desk. He moved toward her with arms out-stretched. "It was all a misunderstanding. I heard the girls talking about us. I thought that you had told..."

She slapped his arms away and stepped backwards. "How dare you think I told? We swore to secrecy. Girls *talk*, that's all. They talk and speculate. But they didn't KNOW." A feverish light glinted in her green eyes.

As the last gasp of self-respect spent itself, he dropped to his knees. "Forgive me. Oh God, Jennifer, please forgive me. I *do* love you."

"I've learned a great lesson from you, *Mr.* Herrick," she said, her voice as cold as ice. There's no such thing as love." Snapping off her flashlight, she turned to leave.

"Don't go. Let me explain," he begged. "My job..."

"Yes," she said, "your job. Well, you don't have me anymore, but you *do* have your job. I hope it keeps you warm on a cold winter's night."

And with that she left him, the door gaping open behind her.

❧

"Kicked out for cheating," Jennifer told the others that morning. Her cavalier attitude belied her bloodshot eyes.

The Corridor Girls stood together at the back door for a few awkward moments repeating promises to write, to be in touch, until Jennifer had to urge them not to make themselves late to class. Bidding them a carefree farewell, she stood alone as she waited for the limo her parents had sent to pick her up.

Dreams, the world, God...all are equal frauds. In the end, we only have ourselves.

She fisted her tears away.

A subdued atmosphere hung over the smoking lounge that evening. It was as if they were strangers thrown together in a waiting room, awkward with one another, not certain what to say. No one even smoked. Normally after exams, the room was filled with the shrill excitement of relief and the giddy foolishness of exhaustion. However, the unexpected shock of Jennifer's abrupt departure had taken its toll. Even prospects of the dance provided them with little distraction.

"Boy, I never saw anything happen so darn fast," Sheila said. "Here one day, gone the next. You just never know about people."

Audrey snorted at Sheila's comment. "I smell a skunk," she said, "and I think its name is Herrick." The girls huddled forward, waiting for Audrey to put into words what they all had been thinking.

"What do you mean?" Karen asked, her usual innocent, wide-eyed expression was clear behind her glasses.

"For Christ's sake," Audrey said, pacing around the lounge, "you idiots know damn well that Jennifer never cheated. So obviously there's some kind of subterfuge going on."

Encouraged both by Audrey and the general agreement, Heather said, "Nancy and I were saying the same thing last night. Jennifer is smart. She never had to study much; I mean she didn't need to cheat. She would have aced that test without it. Besides, I think she was making a real effort lately."

"But if it wasn't cheating, what was it?" Karen asked. "If something like that could happen to her, then all of us are vulnerable."

"Well, Herrick put the finger on her, so it must have been

something to do with the two of them," Audrey said. She shrugged as if the conversation reached a dead end and she couldn't care less about pursuing it further.

Sheila plunged her hands deep into her pockets and to her surprise discovered a forgotten, slightly mashed Reeses Cup. "Did Jennifer say anything last night, Nancy?"

"No," Nancy told her. "Not a word about it." As for her and Mr. Herrick, Jennifer hadn't even mentioned his name in weeks. There was none of that wise talk like the old Jennifer. As a matter of fact, she seemed much more...well, much mellower. "I hate to say it," Nancy continued thoughtfully, "but Audrey could be right. Only I can't imagine why Mr. Herrick would do such a thing."

Wearing a contemptuous expression, Audrey slumped down in a wooden desk chair, stretching her long legs far in front of her. "You've got to give the guy credit. It takes some really outstanding qualities to be able to lie with a clear conscience. He's such a shit. This is also a good indication of the staunch faith the faculty has in us...guilty till proven innocent."

"Maybe there's nothing as vicious as a lover scorned," Sheila suggested around a mouthful of stale peanut butter.

Karen grinned for a moment. "The quote is slightly twisted but the idea could be right if you all remember how Jennifer used to chase him. But Mr. Herrick just doesn't seem like the vindictive type to me. And in all fairness to the faculty, she apparently denied nothing, so what else could they think?"

Nancy leaned forward, her muscles tensed. "Don't tell me that," she said. Her voice was pitched high and her pale face drained of all color. "If the teachers cared enough to find the truth, they would have known that Jennifer was not a cheater. Mr. Herrick is a rat, just like most boys. He's sneaky and sex-crazed, and the rest of the faculty is guilty because they believed his lies."

Nancy was as startled as her audience seemed by her passion. Lowering her voice, she finished her protest lamely. "No questions, no investigation, just, 'get out,' thanks to Herrick. It's not fair!" She kept snapping her Zippo open and shut.

Heather stared at her friend with concern. She hoped the others would not detect the strange violence and personal fear behind Nancy's unexpected outburst.

"We'll never know the truth," Audrey said in disgust, "so you might as well light up a butt and forget Jennifer Stewart. And Mr. Herrick."

The finality of Audrey's sharp voice, threw the girls back into silence. Fortified by their knowledge that Jennifer had been unfairly condemned, they drew close together in solidarity. They were helpless to change the situation, but no one would trust authority again as they once had.

Nancy took a deep drag of her Kool, the tip swelled to an orange glow. She knew that Jennifer had become a hero, a symbol for the girls' own private revolution of distrust and resentment. Jennifer was their armor against authority.

That same evening, Miss Wade gathered her charges for an impromptu meeting. She smiled patiently while The Corridor Girls seated themselves in her small sitting room. She stood, folding the bottom of her long wool bathrobe carefully around her mammoth legs, waiting until the room was quiet.

"I hope you will indulge me with a few moments of your free time," she said, as she paused for dramatic effect, knowing no one would dare to object. "Whether you realize it or not, I am responsible for each one of you, and your actions. I receive praise for your achievements and reproach for your failures. Consequently, you can perhaps appreciate my feelings concerning Jennifer Stewart's blatant disregard for honesty and trust. Her actions cast serious doubts on me and my ability to lead my girls toward maturity and a better life. I know you have heard about what happened in detail from Miss Hicks, so I will not expand on it further. For me, despair is not the answer; I must seek help from above for the knowledge and understanding to guide you through these difficult years."

Her voice quivered and her hands began to tremble. She

took a deep breath. "God's intercession can be powerful and for those who open their hearts to Him, nothing is too insignificant for His attention. It is never too late. My only hope is that the sins of one girl will not visit the rest of you. Such evil contagion could deteriorate the fine progress some of you have made this year."

When the girls began shifting their positions restlessly, Miss Wade paused with a meaningful glance directed at Nancy.

"The forthcoming dance could be a fine opportunity to prove that you truly respect God, and me," she continued, "by conducting yourselves like mature ladies and by upholding the virtues and ideals worthy of loyal students at Winthrop Academy."

The deep red of Miss Wade's bathrobe accented the flush that started to inflame her cheeks as her voice rose to accompany the climax of her speech. When she fell silent, the girls took it as their cue to leave.

"Please feel free to ask me for advice concerning how to act with your dates at the dance," Miss Wade called after them. "Now run along, I will check on you before I retire."

Things were going haywire this term, Miss Wade thought. Jennifer cheating. And now the dance. Her girls had better behave themselves or they'll have her to reckon with. No matter what happened, she would be watching like a hawk.

Later, back in her room, after patrolling the halls for signs of after-hours activity, Miss Wade sank onto her bed and flopped back against her pillows. She felt disgraced and it was all Jennifer's fault. Why had this bright girl shamed herself by such blatant disregard for the rules? And why didn't she admit to cheating?

Miss Wade could barely breathe. She placed her hand on her breast where the nipple was hard and distended. She rubbed it to help it soften; but instead, her place down there began to throb hard and fast. Her mouth opened as though she were about to receive communion and her body arched on the bed while she mutely rode out yet another episode. It was painful. But, oh, such delicious pain.

"Dear God, when will this change of life be over?" she whispered.

Rolling on her side, she thought about Nancy. That dear child. How could she save her with Heather interfering all the time? She decided that she must advise Miss Hicks that it was an unwise decision for those two to room together after vacation. It would be more than Miss Wade could bear if Nancy did not take God into her soul.

Now it was time to shower away the last vestiges of her most recent change of life episode.

Exhaustion hammered Jonathan. He had skipped dinner in the main dining room, and now he poured himself another Scotch, part of which spilled on the floor. Leaning against the cool refrigerator, he gulped the rest with his glasses resting on the tip of his nose. His life had slipped from his grasp and in his desperation, he didn't even know in what direction to reach for it.

She had never said a word. She could have denounced him and she had not. *How could he have been so stupid and cruel to Jennifer? Jennifer. The love of his life?* He recoiled from the sure evil of his deception.

Jonathan had reached a turning point, drunk to sober, a point of decision. Maybe he couldn't reconcile with Jennifer, but he could face up to what he had done.

Suddenly, propelled by a seething desire to unburden his guilt, Jonathan ran up to the main building, charged up the stairs to Miss Hicks' office and pounded on the door.

Under her sardonic eye, his voice dried in his throat. The air thundered between them with the sound of his words as he confessed. She looked at him, incredulous, too stunned to calculate the damage.

Her face sagged with disappointment, "This is a nightmare," she said, shutting her eyes as if to push away his words.

Jonathan did not speak again. He both longed for it to end and dreaded it; in the meantime, there was nothing further he could say.

The silence stretched as Miss Hicks considered him with cold detachment. A small part of her reason for hiring this man had been because he was not handsome, someone who would not present a problem as far as the girls were concerned.

"If only we could foresee the consequences of our choices," Jonathan said sensing that more explanation was needed, "I was too busy obeying the rules of life to question them."

He looked at her expression which blended dislike and something close to naked panic.

"You're through here," she said woodenly. "You know that, don't you?"

She turned away from him, unable to even look at his sinning face. The truth was, she thought, that life was the same everywhere. There was no escape from that reality, and no one was exempt.

But now what would she do about Jennifer? Miss Hicks' anger was laced with fear. What could she tell Jennifer's parents? Because she had to tell them the truth. The truth was fundamental to the ethos of the academy. But more than this, she wondered if her school could survive a scandal of this magnitude.

Jonathan took his cue from the finality in her voice, strangely enough, feeling a great burden slide from his back. He had regained his autonomy. He was free. Free to go to Mexico and, God willing, to find Jennifer.

Outside a fine rain fell, drops spotting his glasses, but his thoughts had already moved away from Winthrop Academy, racing ahead of him, out into the dark.

CHAPTER ELEVEN

The last day of exams, and the wake-like atmosphere following Jennifer's banishment was finally broken. The girls hurried down the corridor, stifling giggles over Miss Wade's wacky advice, especially about the dance.

The remainder of the week had been a flurry of preparation, nervous anticipation filled with last minute diets, beauty treatments and anxious speculation about blind dates. Nancy had different misgivings as the general excitement mounted and Saturday drew near.

Why had she ever agreed to attend the dance, Nancy asked herself over and over again? She knew her experience with Philip shouldn't turn her off boys forever. But she was nervous, especially after the encounter with the Townies. She tried to convince herself that she was not afraid, that she would not end up being another Miss Hicks. Or worse yet, Miss Wade. However, she dreaded the thought of dancing with someone. In this case, she was grateful for Winthrop's strict rules.

Heather said she simply had to overcome her fear and distrust. Heather was so good to her, and she could hardly wait until vacation. She wanted to hold the newest member of the Brock family in her arms. *Rose, they named her, how sweet.* She had hoped it would ease her own loss. There were still so many times that she cried in silence.

"Nancy!" Heather's ebullient voice broke into Nancy's thoughts. "Nancy Walden, where are you? Miss Hicks said that after vacation, she may let me move in with you. We can room together!"

"What? You mean she actually gave us permission? I

can't believe Miss Wade won't veto it. Oh, I'm so happy." The friends circled arms as they danced round and round down the corridor.

"All girls on the dance committee, please rise off your rear ends and get downstairs," Sheila bellowed as she opened the door to Heather's room where the girls were lounging on the floor and the bed.

"Jesus, Sheila, for someone who didn't even want to go to this stupid dance, you sure are getting hot about it," Audrey teased.

"Isn't that the pot calling the kettle black?" Karen laughed and patted the curlers in Audrey's hair.

"Oh go to hell," Audrey replied as she yanked the curlers from her head.

"Come on you guys," Sheila insisted, "they need help setting up the music and the decorations. You can finish your primping later."

"It's only one night out of all the others. I can't see why all the fuss over our appearance." Defying the ritual of pre-dance diets, Sheila peeled the paper from a Heath bar, closing her eyes as she sucked the chocolate off.

"That's obvious." Audrey said smirking and stuffing her curlers into her pocket.

The study hall, stripped of chairs and desks, took on an air of festivity as the girls stretched strings of fairy lights and blue and yellow streamers across the room, creating a second ceiling of woven colors.

Those who had not yet washed their hair rubbed blown up balloons vigorously on their heads. That produced enough static electricity to make the balloons stick on the walls, hiding portraits of Miss Hicks' sober ancestors. A few girls sorted and stacked the popular records on a table next to the record player. Slow numbers should follow each foxtrot and jitterbug.

"Don't forget Miss Hicks' six-inch rule, you sex pots." Sheila laughed as she paraded around the room with two balloons stuck to her head.

"What rule is that?" Nancy looked at Heather.

"Oh, she has to be able to fit a spread-out hand between you and your dancing partner."

"Yeah, you have to leave room for the Holy Ghost," Audrey snickered. "After all, they don't want anyone to get pregnant." Audrey added, remembering too late about Nancy.

Nancy smiled stiffly, as though the joke seemed funny to her.

Sheila clapped her hands. "Well, I don't know about the rest of you debutantes, but, if we're going to come out tonight, we have a lot of work to do on ourselves between now and then."

They took one last look around the converted room, approved their handiwork, and moved as one unit toward the door.

"See you at the ball," Sheila called over her shoulder.

The girls were in a whirl as they transformed themselves for the dance. Some took long showers or lay on their backs with their feet up against the wall to improve their complexions. Others waved their fingers in the air to hasten the drying of fresh nail polish. Pimples were squeezed, hair twirled into pin curls or fat curlers, make-up applied to cover flaws, legs and armpits were shaved, and eyebrows plucked. The air of anticipation ran high throughout the corridor, as well as the rest of the dormitories.

Sheila wrestled into her girdle. It wasn't fair. Everyone else wore a garter belt, but she was fat. Disgusted, she adjusted her dress shields and struggled to pull her pale yellow dress down over her big boobs. Clearly, there had been too many nights of gorging on the food her mother sent every week. *Damn those Heath bars and Mom's double chocolate brownies.* Her short hair looked too kinky when she took out the bobby pins. She brushed it and tried to smooth it down, but she couldn't make it behave. *Great. She'd be a fat, red-headed, frizz-ball tonight.*

Heather went to Nancy's room so they could get ready together. Nancy had foregone Heather's offer to loan her a dress when a gown arrived in the mail from her mother. She was stunned. It was a teal-colored taffeta dress, a *Lanz*...beautiful and modest enough to pass Miss Hicks' test. Perhaps her parents were actually ready to forgive her at last.

"Have you seen the bra and panty set that Eleanor sent me?" Heather asked. "I'd swear it was in the box with my dress."

Nancy shrugged. "They must be around somewhere. You can wear old underwear. No one's going to see it any way."

"I guess you're right." It was obvious to Nancy that Heather was anxious for the evening to begin. "You're so pretty," she told Nancy while watching her brush her long hair until it shone.

"No, I'm not," Nancy said. "You're the pretty one. I always wanted to be a blonde."

"Guess we always want what we don't have, huh?"

"Don't worry; I'm sure the boys will like you...if that's what you want."

Heather smiled. She hoped she would meet a boy she liked. Nothing could take the place of her friendship with Nancy, but it would be fun to have a boyfriend, too. After all, Nancy had had an actual sexual experience with Philip, while Heather had never even been kissed! Well, not French kissed, anyway.

Heather wore an organdy dress fitted at the waist with a full crinoline slip underneath that made it stand out. The gown matched the indigo of her eyes. She twirled around the room, starting to feel the excitement of the evening.

"I wonder if I'll meet Mr. Perfect," Heather said, smiling at herself in the mirror.

Nancy was irritated by Heather's interest in boys. Didn't she realize how awful they could be?

"Oh, Nance," Heather said reacting to the look on her face, "not every boy is going to be like Philip."

"I know," Nancy conceded. "But most of the boys will

probably be jerks. Or worse, like those Townies." Nancy cringed at the thought.

"You gotta let that go. They're history."

"I guess you're right. It's just that so much has happened, and, well, I'm nervous about tonight."

Heather grabbed Nancy's hands and swung her around the room. "When we get back from vacation, we'll be roommates. I can't wait!"

"Me too."

Miss Hicks had said that all bra straps had to be fully covered, and strapless gowns were forbidden because, well, they were too provocative. That was fine with her, Nancy thought, as she adjusted the cap sleeves of her teal gown. If it weren't for Heather, she wouldn't be going to the dance at all. She would much rather have curled up in bed and read a good book. It occurred to her that she could have, since her roommate was gone.

"You know," she said, "I still can't believe Jennifer was expelled."

"It just doesn't make any sense," Heather agreed. "Maybe she had to leave school for some other reason."

Nancy gasped. "You mean Jennifer might be pregnant?"

Heather shook her head. "No, she was bumming a tampax just a few days ago, so I know she had the curse. But I do wonder where she is. Do you think she's all right?"

"Knowing Jennifer, I'm sure she is," Nancy told her.

But actually, she was not that sure...not that sure at all.

Finally, each girl left her room, transformed into a young lady. Some staggered a bit, wearing their dyed-to-match high heels for the first time. Walking down the corridor, Nancy listened as they discussed how to ditch a date, how to kiss a guy with braces and what to do if your date acted horny. Karen urged them to remember that a guy will think you're great if you get him to talk about himself.

That certainly would be the best defense, Nancy told herself.

There was an uneasy quiet as the girls, drawn into the atmosphere of mutual expectation, swarmed into the transformed study hall where the colored lights twinkled, casting a soft romantic glow. Members of the decorating committee were gratified by the sighs and exclamations of the other girls.

The boys from the Bryant School stood in a row against the wall. Nancy observed that they looked as uncomfortable and anxious as the girls. There were short ones and tall ones. Some were pimply and some handsome. Some had unruly hair and others had theirs plastered with Brylcream. Heather gave Nancy a 'this-is-going-to-be-interesting' look as they walked in with the other girls.

Miss Hicks separated herself from a group of chaperones. She was wearing a copper colored, long-sleeved satin gown with a mandarin collar. Her grandmother's Victorian earrings matched perfectly. The girls referred to her attire as Miss Hicks' "spring dance uniform."

"Winthrop Academy would like to welcome our guests from the Bryant School," she announced.

Everyone clapped. The girls giggled, while the boys' faces turned red.

"Boys and girls," Miss Hicks continued, "we want you to have a lovely evening. Using the information you all submitted, the dance committees from both schools have matched each of you with a blind date. Mr. Herrick...uh, I mean Mr. Packer will call out your names and you may meet in front of the fire place. There you may shake hands with your date for the evening. Don't forget, you may cut in on the dance floor if you wish to change partners, if everyone involved mutually consents, that is. Remember, God is watching over us tonight as He always does. So, respect one another, don't dance close, and have a good time."

That was one of Miss Hicks' rules that Nancy thoroughly agreed with!

When someone started the record player and Patti Page

began to croon *Old Cape Cod,* one couple after another moved out onto the dance floor, some awkward, some more self-assured. But all of them were trying to make conversation, despite sweaty hands, bad breath, pimples, and acute self-consciousness. As a backup, the girls, and probably the boys too, had planned secret signals if they wanted to swap partners.

Nancy couldn't imagine why she had agreed to go to this dance, but knew she might as well make the most of it at this point. After Mr. Packer called her name, a stocky, blue-eyed boy with dark curly hair had approached her. "Hi," he said, "my name is Randy Gilbert. I think I'm your date."

Nancy was so nervous that her hands were shaking. "I guess you're right," she said, "I'm the one you're stuck with."

Awkwardly, he put his arm around her waist and they began to dance to Pat Boone's *Love Letters in the Sand.* Randy was slow and clumsy. She looked over at Heather, dancing with a red-headed freckle-faced kid who definitely held her attention. Nancy felt curiously apart for a moment, alone and very small, unsure of what lay ahead. As if sensing this, Heather caught her eye, begging her to hold on, and in return, Nancy gave a sign that all was okay. If she had to be at the dance, then Randy would do as well as anyone, although in reality Nancy felt like a misfit among all the other giggling teenagers. The sad longing of the music stole into her thoughts. In a situation like this, with its overtones of romance, her past set her apart, and made her feel as if she were a hundred years old.

Sheila waltzed by with a good looking, football type. Poor girl, it looked like he was trying to signal his buddies behind her back although Sheila was, as usual, oblivious, chatting away.

Was she actually trying that idea of Jennifer's...that stroking a guy's neck gave him a hard on? Was that her tongue? Jesus, she's acting like an idiot. Audrey shook her head and lost the beat, stepping on her date's foot.

All around the dance floor, strangers held one another and tried to make small-talk. Their voices rose above Jimmie Rodgers singing *Kisses Sweeter than Wine*, but the lyrics lingered in Nancy's mind. She was melancholy because they made her think of Jennifer, and that surprised her. *Where was her roommate?* Had she simply disappeared forever inside that limousine? Was she happy or was she feeling as lost as Nancy knew herself to be?

The room was filled with laughter. Nancy felt as though this was a world in which she was no longer a part. Casual comments flitted around the room.

"You come from?"

"Really? I spent a million summers there."

"Then, you must know..."

"I always vacation in Europe. "

"You skied Aspen, too?"

"Where are you applying? Vassar? Dartmouth?"

"Oh you must be a brain."

The next song plopped down on the turntable and Elvis Presley picked up the pace with; All *Shook Up,* as the girls scanned the dance cards that hung from their wrists. Who would be the next dance partner?

Nancy wished she had signed up for the refreshment committee. Then she'd have an excuse to leave Randy so he could dance with someone else, and she could help serve the punch.

Next to the refreshment table, chaperones from both schools watched the students with an intensity that barely covered their covert interest in one another.

As Miss Hicks prayed that the evening would pass without incident, someone put *The Twelfth of Never* by Johnny Mathis on the turntable. Generally, these dances between Winthrop Academy and the Bryant School went off without a hitch, but now and then, a couple would sneak out to the garden before intermission to do God knew what. After having had to expel Jennifer and dismiss Mr. Herrick, Miss Hicks trusted that nothing else disastrous would happen. The horror of having to tell the girls about Mr. Herrick weighed heavily. She must not think about this now.

Raising her hand to her face, she drew in the lemon scent of the furniture polish that had, over the years, smoothed the cherry wood arms of the chair she was sitting in to a fine patina.

Glancing around the room, she saw Miss Wade, whose posture was stiff as the proverbial board. Sam, on the other hand, was nowhere in sight.

Miss Wade stood by the wall, praying silently to God to forgive these children for their sins. They were dancing too close. The boys with their pocketknives, pressing them against the girls' legs as if they could not wait to take their dates outside where they would do crazy things. Young girls had no idea about boys' audacity. Most of them probably didn't know what that bulge was that was pushing into them.

Heat suddenly engulfed her. The throbbing of her blood felt like a jack-hammer in her brain. Her eyes dulled, then widened in a moment of frozen terror. No. No, please don't let this happen here! Please, dear God!

Miss Wade's sexual center softened and swelled until it burst open. She felt wetness between her legs. She took a deep breath, filled her lungs until they might burst and pushed against the sensations. She glanced around, assuring herself that no one had noticed her hot flash episode, and then she headed for the staff lounge.

She decided to have a meeting with the girls tomorrow after vespers. They must ask God to forgive them for lusting after these boys.

Between records, Nancy went to the ladies' room where she was joined by the other Corridor Girls, their skirts rustling as they pressed three deep in front of the bathroom mirror to renew lipstick and compare notes.

"My date is a very nice guy from Boston," Karen said, her green eyes sparkling. "In fact, he sort of reminds me of my brothers. He's so easy to talk to and of course, he loves the Red Sox. And, he didn't even drop his arms from around my waist when the music died." Without her glasses, she had to squint to see herself in the mirror.

"Well, fancy you meeting someone nice," Audrey said. "My date is a bore. Can you imagine? He was using the breathe-in-the-ear technique! A complete spastic and he has halitosis, too. Someone should have put saltpeter in his punch."

"I think I'm in love with Darren," Sheila said as she tried to smooth her curls. "He's a real hunk and I swear he was looking down the front of my dress."

"But, does *he* like *you*?" It takes two to tango, you know," Audrey asked. "Frankly, I think he looks like a sex fiend in that green jacket."

"I *think* he likes me," Sheila said. "He hasn't exactly tried to get rid of me."

Nancy noticed the pain in Sheila's eyes that belied her words. "Don't worry, Sheila," she said, I'm sure he likes you. Just remember, guys can be real horse's asses, so don't lose your head over this preppy goon."

Heather grabbed Nancy by the arm and guided her to a corner of the ladies' room. "Nance, what do you think about my date, Aaron? He's really swift, isn't he?"

"I don't know, Heather. Do you like him? That's the important thing."

"Absolutely! He said that he might come and visit us at my house during summer vacation."

"Well, don't get too excited," Nancy warned her, "boys can disappoint you. Just be careful."

"Oh, Nance, you worry too much. By the way, I noticed that you gave me the signal. You must like your date, too."

"Randy? Oh, he's okay," Nancy said. "He's better than

some and I don't have to make conversation. All I have to do is listen."

The truth was, Nancy wanted to go back to her room and get into her pajamas. She didn't want that eager beaver that Heather was dancing with to come and visit them this summer. She just wanted to spend the time alone with Heather and her family. And baby Rose. This guy would ruin everything. He didn't know Heather. He hadn't been through any of the things the two of them had in building a friendship.

At that moment, Nancy was more isolated than ever before. Seeing her best friend giggling over a boy disappointed her. She thought there had been less than Miss Hicks' six inches between them. Didn't Heather know he would end up hurting her? Lord, she had shared everything with her, and it hadn't even registered.

Some of the girls were flustered, some bored. Some thought they were falling in love. But they all returned from the bathroom, their dance cards discarded, a move that made many partners happy and a few who were sitting down, desperate to escape.

Outside the double French doors leading to the patio, Mr. Jones stood in the shadows with his hat pulled low. Sweat beaded his forehead as he watched the young couples glide across the dance floor. No one noticed him.

The minute the last bus filled with rowdy boys pulled away from the school, the girls kicked off their shoes, and ran up the stairs to their rooms to compare notes. Most girls were relieved, but some had stars in their eyes. Everyone had a tale to tell. At last the corridor was silent. Gowns, garter belts, and stockings draped over chairs or in pools on the floor were the only evidence left of the long-anticipated evening.

At Winthrop Academy, the girls are allowed to skip breakfast after a dance, so of course nobody got up until almost noon. The afternoon passed quickly as they exchanged stories about their dates, most centered on how pathetic and pimply they were. Only Heather and Karen had anything nice to say.

Sunday night after vespers, Miss Hicks presented her annual tirade about the conduct of *some* ladies at the dance, while Miss Wade nodded agreement, and looked around for her Corridor Girls to give them each a significant look. Miss Hicks took up the polemic by calling the behavior of some of the student body: “Common, coarse, crude, cheap, crass, vulgar and smutty.” The girls, having heard her discourse many times before, sat in a conspiracy of silence.

CHAPTER TWELVE

"Which bin are your suitcases in, Nance?" Heather called as she rushed down the corridor. "I'm going to the basement for mine. I'll get yours at the same time."

"I brought mine up this morning, but thanks anyway."

Heather skipped down the back stairs, through the long hallway, past the kitchen, then on to the door leading to the basement where each girl stored suitcases and sport equipment. As she walked down the stairs and through the furnace room to reach the bins, her eyes adjusted slowly to the fractured light. She came to an abrupt stop, unable to believe her eyes. There was the shapeless figure of Mr. Jones with a pair of silky underpants pressed against his stubbled face. At first, when she peered through the darkness that separated them, she thought it was sort of funny. But then she saw that his fly was open, and he was playing with his *thing*. Shocked, she found herself unable to move.

She watched The Creep as he stuffed the panties into his mouth. He threw his head back and bellowed. The sound was like the roar of a goaded bull. He flung his arms out, shaking all over as his penis swelled and grew deep purple. And then there was only the sound of his ragged breathing. It filled the room. The shadows from the furnace-glow played along the walls and the stench of The Creep was overwhelming.

Heather heard herself shriek, "Oh my God!" her last shred of control shattering. The noise spiraled around the room.

Mr. Jones froze when he heard Heather's scream. His watery red-rimmed eyes blinked in the semi darkness. His hand dropped to his side and wrapped around the furnace poker as though it was placed there to protect him.

Seeing this, Heather turned and ran to the stairs, gripping the rail. Her palm froze against the metal. Hysteria clogged her throat when she tried to call for help.

The Creep lunged forward, faster than she had ever seen him move, and he grasped her free arm, yanking her backward. Then he stumbled, losing his grip, leaving Heather to half crawl half run back toward the stairs, her breath a terrible weight in her chest.

His howl resonated off the walls and then hissed like a punctured balloon. She felt it pierce her body and alter the rhythm of her heart. As she began to scramble up the stairs again, he grabbed her ankle and then he struck her.

When Heather saw the poker raised above her again and again, she felt herself disintegrate. She closed her eyes and cringed in anticipation of the next blow. One second. Five seconds. Maybe he had stopped. Hope rose, only to be dashed when the poker slammed into her one last time.

Slowly Mr. Jones got to his feet. He dropped the poker as though he had reached into the flames of the furnace, and the heat had seared it permanently into his flesh.

He stared at Heather's inert body. Her eyes were pooled with blood. Now she was no longer the pretty polite girl who always said, "Hello, Mr. Jones," in the hallways. He had liked her; she had been kind to him. His body shook, his face turned hideous with the horror of what he had done.

But it was not really his fault. It was *her* fault, coming down here when she did. *The stupid girl*. Unable to look at her any longer, he took her arms and dragged her behind the boiler where he arranged her limbs straight and decent, then pulled her skirt down carefully. He wiped his bloody hands on his pants. Then through his daze, the need to escape overpowered him.

What would his sister say? What would she do to him?

You've been bad. So bad. They were words he had heard all his life. Except from Beth. His sister loved him no matter what. She had made a home for him here. And now look what he'd done.

Mr. Jones swayed toward a wooden door in the corner of the basement. Pushing it open with his shoulder, he entered his secret sanctum. There, draped around the room was underwear from the past twenty years, stolen from the girls' closets and drawers, from under their beds, or from a shower rod where they had been left to dry. Lacy panties of all sizes, some pink, some white, and some black, all so luscious and smooth. Lurching from side to side, he snatched his prizes off the walls, and he clutched them to his chest. Burying his face in them, he broke into sobs.

Miss Wade was determined to have a serious talk with Heather before vacation to explain why she was against her rooming with Nancy. Of course, she wouldn't come right out and say that Heather would be a negative influence on her protégée. She'd merely point out that Nancy needed a stronger connection with God because she had been through so much. Naturally, she wouldn't refer to the baby. It should be enough just to make a few veiled references to the tragedy. In the afternoon, she made her way along the corridor, calling Heather's name.

"She's not here, Miss Wade," Nancy told her. "She went to the basement to get her suitcases about an hour ago, and then she was planning to see her counselor. We've both applied to Wellesley, Miss Wade, won't that be great?'

"Never mind about that, Nancy, I need to talk to her right now."

"Or, maybe she's in the smoking lounge. I'll take a look."

"I'll go with you," Miss Wade said. Clearly, she was on a mission.

Finding no one in Sheila's room or the smoking lounge,

Miss Wade asked Nancy to check the basement while she looked in the library. The sound of her heavy legs rubbing together receded while Nancy went in the opposite direction.

As Nancy entered the basement, she was struck by a distinct sense that something was wrong. Perhaps it was an odor. Or the eerie stillness of the room. It could even have been because the door had been wide open. Or maybe because Mr. Jones spent a lot of time down there. Whatever it was, she felt uneasy.

"Heather! Heather," she called out, squinting into the half-lit room. Nancy started to check the storage bins around the other side of the furnace and then hesitated. If Heather were there she would have answered her. She peeked around the furnace, and saw Heather's body looking as if it would rise from sleep. Except for the blood where the poker had smashed her head.

"Oh Lord. Oh Lord God. Oh my good Christ, no!"

Nancy stumbled backwards lurching against the wall, shaking her head in abject disbelief. Then her voice broke the silence taking on a feral quality as she sprang forward again to where Heather lay.

"What happened, Heather?" she cried, wringing her hands. "What happened to you?" Her long hair lightly brushed Heather's cheek when she leaned closer to look at her. A shiver passed through her and then she stood upright, staring blindly.

A sob spiraled up in her throat like a scalding splash of acid as she heard a hoarse cry. Then she saw Mr. Jones through the open door, his face buried in something that looked like underwear.

Oh my God, those look like Heather's panties, the ones Eleanor sent her for the dance...

Trembling violently, Nancy turned and bolted up the basement steps, careening along the hallway where the Corridor Girls had laughed their way to the kitchen not so long ago.

Bursting into Heather's room, she slammed the door behind her and climbed into Heather's bed, retreating into its folds.

Mr. Jones knew what he had to do. He grabbed a can of paint thinner, opened it, and shook its contents erratically around the room, emptying it onto his precious collection of panties. One last time, he hugged them to his chest and burrowed his face in their softness. With final resolve, he thrust them again to the floor, lit a match and dropped it. He screamed with remorse. The fire jumped to his pant legs, and moved steadily across his chest. Oblivious to the smell of scorching skin, he drew his fingers over his eyes, turned away, and stumbled up the cellar stairs leaving a trail of smoldering silk behind him. Passing through the door that led to the outside, he fled wildly toward the soccer field. A human torch, Mr. Jones disappeared down a path that led him deep into the woods.

Miss Hicks stood in the middle of her sitting room. Having talked with Sam about Jonathan's confession, she felt that perhaps all was not lost. A nerve twanged at the base of her skull. "Truth has a life of its own," she muttered aloud.

She steeled herself against self-pity. Sam had said she must pull herself together, that his lie could be dealt with without risking the future of the academy. All that was needed was an honest explanation. Maybe a full tuition refund to Jennifer's parents. An apology to the entire student body. Perhaps a lesson could be made of this. Miss Hicks strove for composure. Composure and a plan.

It was at this moment that she heard hysterical cries coming from downstairs and outside her window. She was already dealing with the worst thing that she could ever have imagined might happen to her school, and now girls were screaming.

What's going on? Loud voices aren't allowed in the building. Why am I hearing loud voices? Fear made her heart race.

Hilda Sampson rushed from her office and grabbed Miss Hicks' arm. "What is it, Beth? What's all the commotion?"

"I don't know, we've got to get down there Sam and find out." Apprehension climbed the back of her neck as she hurried down the stairs, Sam close by her side.

Miss Hicks felt a wall of dread caving in around her, and her beloved Academy, too.

The entire student body was in an uproar. Their voices surged in cross currents as they stood huddled in small groups in the driveway and cried and hugged each other. It was bedlam with a background of fire alarms screeching next to the annex. A black choking smoke billowed out of the annex basement and from the corridor windows, which were directly above.

The firemen were dousing the main building with water and chemicals. It was saved, but the fire chief said the annex would be a total loss. They had pulled Heather's charred beaten body out of the furnace room. When the chief had unzipped the black body bag inside the ambulance for Miss Hicks to view what was there, she staggered and would have fainted if Sam had not supported her. The fire chief physically pushed the two women away from the ambulance.

"Take all the girls inside," he shouted. "*Now*. The main building is clear."

An unnatural calm descended upon Miss Hicks. *They were still her girls. They needed her*. She herded them back into the building, trying to soothe and console them.

Sheila and Audrey were sobbing, holding on to each other. Karen was leaning against Sheila's back, crying uncontrollably.

Miss Hicks patted Karen's shoulder as she spoke to Sam around the cluster of Corridor Girls. "Where is Gertrude? I need her to take a head count, especially for the annex."

"God only knows."

Miss Hicks raised her voice over the din to announce that all the parents would be contacted to arrange for immediate travel plans or accommodations at the hotel in town. She was almost shouting when she called for a head count, but no one was listening.

❧

A charge exploded in Nancy's mind, succeeded by profound darkness. Something remained in her memory, something perhaps not seen but merely imagined. She was nothing without Heather, a shadow creeping under the sunshine.

Then, a surge of power outside her ability to think pushed her to her feet and down the smoky corridor. Her arms were extended, and her lips were pinched into a purple wound.

"Help me, God, help me!" she sobbed and slumped to the floor as Miss Wade opened her door.

Nancy yielded before the solid figure, everything else slid away.

❧

While Miss Hicks and Sam tried to calm the shocked grief-stricken girls in the reception hall, Miss Wade was still in the annex sitting on her bed with Nancy's head in her lap. Strands of Nancy's silken skein of black hair were strewn about them like flowers on a grave. Miss Wade held a pair of scissors in hand.

"Nancy, you are pure and clean as the angels of heaven, given to us by God as a gift of love," Miss Wade prayed aloud. "Whatever has happened is surely the work of the devil."

A flush spread down her neck as she spoke. "Satan walks among us and he takes many forms. He may try to look like us and he may try to act like us, but he is not one of us. We must always be on our guard, my dearest child, ready to ward off his evil whenever and wherever we encounter it. We must protect ourselves and our loved ones from him." Waves of emotion rose in Miss Wade, cresting to engulf them both.

Crushing Nancy's shorn head to her breast, Miss Wade rocked her in her arms as a fireman burst into the room.

Miss Hicks paused for a moment in front of the French doors in the reception hall, her back to the melee and confusion. She ran her hand lovingly over the paneling with its intricate carving. The air was heavy with the aroma of lemon oil and smoke. She clasped both hands behind her back.

She already knew in her heart that her brother was responsible for Heather's death, as well as for the fire. Now Paul would be put away permanently. She wept for him, the brother whom she had protected all these years. She had given him the name of Mr. Jones so that no one there would make the connection between them. Now he would live in an institution forever, or worse...he could be executed.

This is it, she thought, as the girls finally assembled behind her. She was finished, just like Herrick, only worse. After everything she had done for Winthrop Academy, her career was destroyed. No one would remember her accomplishments. No one would remember how she had cared for each girl who had been committed to her custody over these many years.

Miss Hicks looked up at the portrait of her grandmother Elizabeth, and then at Sam, who was standing at the head of the stairs. Both women were crying bitterly.

CHAPTER THIRTEEN

During the weeks that followed Heather's death, Nancy was lost in the sheer agony of grief. Now that she was back in her parent's house, she felt a sense of isolation, a pain that seemed permanent. Even Joannie tried to talk to her. But how could she explain that the loss of Heather had changed her life forever, how her friendship with Heather had given her courage and confidence and new expectations?

As for her mother, for the first time Nancy thought that she was trying to understand her. The silences that used to sit like a block of ice between them started to melt away. Nancy knew that Heather would have wanted this to happen, and it made it easier for Nancy to complete her course work at home for her diploma.

In a way, it came as no surprise to Nancy when Heather's stepmother wrote to ask if she would join them at a cottage they had rented on Cape Cod for the summer. Not waiting for a response, Eleanor called the next day.

"Harold and I, and Rose, too, really want you," she said. "We need you to be with us. We're falling apart without Heather. Her father's heart is broken." She had chosen her words carefully, as if she considered them fragile, easily misunderstood. "Please say you'll come to us."

Nancy had rolled Eleanor's words around in her mind, savoring them with a lucidity that lies beyond grief.

"Thank you, Eleanor," she said, "I want to come," her voice

so small, it was more a breeze than a sound. Suddenly, she was flooded with wanting.

During that golden summer on Cape Cod, Nancy came to know the warmth of Heather's parents and the consolation and pure joy of caring for Rosie, a natural joy that was somehow as familiar as sunrise.

In August, she heard from, of all people, Audrey, who told her that she was spending the summer at Sheila's house and that it was the greatest. Sheila's brother was a blast and that she, Audrey, had put on twelve pounds!

But the letter from Jennifer gave Nancy the greatest pleasure. It seemed that Mr. Herrick had somehow earned her forgiveness. She wrote that they were looking for a university where he could teach and she could continue her studies.

Nancy held baby Rose as if she were an armful of flowers, fragrant and precious. She was carrying on the life that Heather had bequeathed her.

A light of hope entered her eyes like a timid guest.

EPILOGUE

December 1959

He murdered her.

Gripping the dusty banister with arthritic fingers, Miss Hicks shuffled up the winding staircase. "*Jennifer, Karen, Sheila, Audrey...*" She repeated each one of the girls' names as if they were beads on a rosary. A personal rosary because they had been hers, hadn't they? In *her* school, *her* charges, *her* responsibility. Miss Hicks: headmistress of the most desirable preparatory school in Connecticut.

Betrayal and lies.

Above her, the austere portrait of her grandmother stared down at her in judgment. "I tried to keep it a secret about Paul, Grandmère," she said, pausing to look up at her. "My God, I tried so hard for all those years. Can you ever forgive me?"

Heat, like ribbons of silk, wrapped around her as she entered her room, her rolled-down stockings resting like donuts around her ankles. From the window, she looked down at the sickly elms that flanked the circular drive, and what remained of the extensive gardens now tangled with weeds and neglect. To the west was the deserted athletic building. She remembered so well the year they had raised the funds to build it. "Our alumni were loyal, weren't they Sam," she said, forgetting that Sam's heart had given out not long after the fire.

Outside, night fell and pressed up against the window.

"*Jennifer, Nancy, Heather....*" Her ruinous disgrace.

"I could do it again, Sam," she murmured, "create a whole new school...if you were at my side."

Lying on the rumpled bed, she closed her eyes and felt the weight of darkness on her eyelids. Black wings brushed her face.

"*Murdered*," she whispered as the lead blanket of sleep enveloped her.

READING GROUP GUIDE

Questions for Discussion

1. The novel begins with the opening line: "All her life, Nancy had wanted to make people love her by trying to please them." What expectations about the novel did this establish regarding Nancy? What did it suggest about the eventual outcome of the story?

2. How did Nancy's mother destroy her self-esteem and how did Heather help restore it? Did Nancy's depression hold her back from expressing her true reaction to Jennifer openly talking about sex? Was this part of her disgust over Mr. Herrick?

3. Whether justified or not, Nancy, Jennifer and Heather were sent to Winthrop Academy by their parents for behavior modification. How did their respective family histories determine their behavior and interactions with one another? Why do you think Miss Hicks accepted Nancy mid-year?

4. Was Heather's reaction to her mother's death believable? Is death so different from divorce? How did Nancy help Heather accept her stepmother? Do you think Nancy became too dependent on Heather for validation and support?

5. As headmistress, Miss Hicks followed the antiquated traditions established by her grandmother, but was she

really attuned to the needs of the girls? Was the relationship between her and Sam implied by the author to have lesbian overtones or were they "maiden ladies" who were merely colleagues and friends? Do you see Miss Hicks as a tragic character with the burden of her brother and living up to standards set by her grandmother? Have boarding schools today transcended the old mores?

6. What impact did Nancy and Heather's encounter with the five Townies have on their friendship? Why did Nancy fear lesbian tendencies? Was this a general taboo of the times or was the author suggesting another failing on the part of Miss Hicks, i.e. her relationship with Sam and its possible influence on the students?

7. Jennifer transitioned from flirting to love and as she did, her personality changed. Did Jonathan change in the same way? Did you see him as a letch or someone who finally found his love? Jonathan's betrayal of Jennifer was shocking. Why did he jump to such a quick conclusion? Did you pity him or hate him for his betrayal?

8. Miss Wade followed her own misguided interpretation of God's will. Was she delusional or simply a product of the dogma of the 50s? Why did she pursue Nancy so persistently? Did you think Nancy had any suspicion as to her bizarre "change of life" episodes? What was your response to them? Were you surprised that Nancy turned to her in her moment of terror?

9. The kitchen raid, the dance, the smoking lounge discussions, the resentment toward authority and control, all amplified the conventions of the 50s and were elements that contributed to the bonding of the Corridor Girls, yet they were still antagonistic in hurtful ways. Is this natural among teenagers? Do you think Miss Hicks' "Words to Live By" are truisms that are relevant today?

10. Did The Creep's behavior throughout the book foreshadow his final actions? Did you suspect the filial relationship? Was Miss Hicks wrong not to acknowledge it? Was Nancy's fear of Mr. Jones predictive? Do you think there was a reason the author did not tell the reader if Mr. Jones survived the fire? Did it matter to the story?

11. Did you have trouble relating to the naïveté of teenage girls in the 1950s? Was Nancy's innocence believable even after having had a baby? The diversity between the girls' sexuality was extreme although they were all looking for love. Nancy didn't get the kind of love she wanted from her parents or her sister and although she thought she had gotten it from her boyfriend, in the end, even he had disappointed her. How do you foresee Nancy's ability to have a normal heterosexual relationship?

12. Did you feel that Nancy matured enough from her state of shame and the loss of her soul mate Heather, to function successfully in college?

13. If *Silent Cry* were made into a movie, which Hollywood actors would you envision taking the major roles? Send suggestions to the author at: silentcrynovel@yahoo.com

If you wish to write a review of *Silent Cry*, please go to: *Silent Cry* on: www.amazon.com and then scroll down to: "write an online review".

Made in the USA